The soft footsteps continued up the wall outside the bedroom door. In a moment, D.J. heard them start across the ceiling toward his bed! They passed over the bed and down the wall behind the headboard toward the window.

D.J. couldn't stand it any longer! He swung the boot behind his shoulder, holding it cocked to smash forward while he groped for the light on his nightstand. He switched it on.

The wall was exactly the same as when he'd turned out the light a few hours ago—except—the footsteps continued.

D.J. heard the window slide up. He heard it clearly. But with the light on, he could see the window hadn't moved!

LEE RODDY is a best-selling author of more than 50 books. He lives in the Sierra Nevada Mountains of California and devotes his time to writing books and public speaking. He is a co-writer of the book which became the TV series, "The Life and Times of Grizzly Adams."

Born on an Illinois farm and reared on a California ranch, Lee Roddy grew up around hunters and trail hounds. As a boy, he began writing animal stories. He spent lots of time reading about dogs, horses, and other animals. These stories shaped his thinking and values before he went to Hollywood to write professionally. His Christian commitment later turned his writing talents to books like this one.

This is the eighth book in the D.J. Dillon Adventure Series.

Ghost of the Moaning Mansion

LEE RODDY

THE D.J. DILLON ADVENTURE SERIES

THE HAIR-PULLING BEAR DOG
THE BEAR CUB DISASTER
DOOGER, THE GRASSHOPPER HOUND
THE GHOST DOG OF STONEY RIDGE
MAD DOG OF LOBO MOUNTAIN
THE LEGEND OF THE WHITE RACCOON
THE MYSTERY OF THE BLACK HOLE MINE
GHOST OF THE MOANING MANSION
THE SECRET OF MAD RIVER
ESCAPE DOWN THE RAGING RAPIDS

7 8 9 10 11 12 13 14 Printing/Year 00 99 98 97

Library of Congress Catalog Card Number: 87-81029
ISBN: 1-56476-509-1

Printed in the United States of America

Chariot Books is an imprint of ChariotVictor Publishing,
a division of Cook Communications, Colorado Springs, Colorado 80918
Cook Communications, Paris, Ontario
Kingsway Communications, Eastbourne, England

CONTENTS

To
Ben and Mary Jean Jennings
For pastoring, teaching, and friendship
that helped me step out in faith.

Chapter One

TROUBLE FROM TWO SOURCES

If D.J. Dillon had guessed what a scary, spooky experience was ahead, he wouldn't have scoffed when he heard what his grandfather said.

"Yes sirree! I'm a'going to catch that there ghost—or whatever it is—and make it plumb sorry it ever started scaring decent folks again!"

D.J. and Mrs. Keene, his eighth-grade teacher at Stoney Ridge Grammar School, were sitting on an old couch at Grandpa Dillon's small rented house out in the country. The boy's father had driven Mrs. Keene and D.J. out to see Grandpa. Dad Dillon was now outside splitting firewood by the back door.

There was still a week of vacation left between Christmas and the new year. The weather was clear and crisp at the 3,500-foot elevation of California's Sierra Nevada Mountains, with some snow on the ground.

"Grandpa," the tall, slender thirteen-year-old boy

said through stifled laughter, "since there are no *real* ghosts, how're you going to catch one?"

Grandpa Dillon was a feisty little man who once had been known for having an ornery streak as wide as a barn door. He was slightly stoop-shouldered from years of plowing, but his eyes were bright and teasing behind the wire-rimmed bifocals.

"I know that, and you know that—but does the ghost know it?"

Mrs. Ouida (pronounced "Oh-WEE-Dah") Keene adjusted her glasses on her nose and got up. D.J. thought she had probably been pretty when she was young. She had married late, never had a child, and had been a widow for the last five years. She and Grandpa had grown up together back in Oklahoma.

In her thirty-fifth year of teaching at Stoney Ridge's two-room grammar school, Mrs. Keene was small as a dried up apple core. Her brown eyes showed the strain she'd been under. D.J. remembered when her short hair was brownish-gray, but now it was almost the color of pure silver. She walked toward the window and looked out over the mountains. D.J. thought she could probably see his father splitting firewood because D.J. could hear the maul hitting the oak.

"Now, Caleb," she said, "you mustn't tease D.J. about such things! One of the favorite pastimes of the pioneers was telling tall tales. This is just one of them!"

"You just hold on there a second, Ouida! Something mighty peculiar is going on at that spooky old mansion you bought at Devil's Law—and I'm a'going to find out what it is!"

Grandpa shoved himself to his feet with the aid of a cane he called an "Irish shilellagh."* It skidded on the faded print linoleum floor and the old man almost fell.

D.J. leaped up and grabbed a thin arm. "You OK, Grandpa?"

"Reckon so, D.J." The old man lifted the cane and tipped the end so the boy and the woman could see. "Rubber tip's split. Front part busted open so the wood hits this slick linoleum. Next time I go to town, I'll get a new tip."

"You were saying, Caleb?" the teacher prompted just as she did in history class where D.J. was having a hard time.

"I was a'saying, Ouida, that I don't know how you're so down-right sure this ghost—or whatever it is—isn't real. Didn't you tell me last Sunday at church that some people claimed to have seen it? And lots of folks *heard* it! Didn't you say that?"

"As a Christian woman, I don't believe in ghosts or anything like that! I know you don't either, so stop teasing D.J.! I was merely explaining what's being said and what's been happening lately!"

D.J. shook his blond hair away from his blue eyes. "Mrs. Keene, you said most people had forgotten about the ghost until recently."

"Exactly, D.J.! It was only a legend sometimes written up in the Timbergold County Historical Society's newsletters. That is, until shortly after I invested my life's savings in that mansion.

*You can find an explanation of the starred words under "Life in Stoney Ridge" on pages 120–125.

"I thought it would make a delightful bed and breakfast inn! But who's going to stay in a hundred-year-old mansion supposedly haunted by a Chinese ghost?"

Even though Stoney Ridge School had no retirement program or pension for teachers, everyone knew Mrs. Keene had saved enough that she planned to retire next June. She intended to move 1,500 feet lower down the Sierras to the Mother Lode* country. That's where the California Gold Rush had taken place in the early 1850s.

There a mansion had been built outside the town of Devil's Law. Mrs. Keene had bought the place about a year before.

Many Mother Lode towns had funny names, like Bed Bug, Rough and Ready, and Hangtown. In the early days, many such communities were lawless. But it was said that one was worse than all the others—that it had no law except Satan's. So that place was called Devil's Law.

Grandpa Dillon ran a blue-veined hand, thin and brown-spotted from age, across his chin. "That's why I told you I'd go over and have a look-see, Ouida. It's the least an old friend can do for a purty schoolmarm."

Mrs. Keene sputtered, "Caleb, you haven't changed a bit since we were children. So don't you start giving me any of your blarney! Anyway, I wouldn't let you do it except that maybe an outsider like you might see something I've overlooked."

D.J. studied the two people with curiosity. They were among his favorite people. It was sort of strange, knowing these two adults had been friends for fifty years or more.

The boy had heard the story often enough. Mrs. Keene had left the small Oklahoma farming community and gone on to college. Caleb Dillon had been forced to drop out of grammar school to help his parents, who were tenant farmers.

Grandpa and Mrs. Keene hadn't seen each other for many years. Then she returned to Oklahoma for the twenty-fifth reunion of her high school's graduation class. She was then a teacher in Stoney Ridge, California. She had invited Caleb and his wife to come visit someday.

When Grandma Dillon died, Grandpa talked his son and daughter-in-law into visiting Stoney Ridge. Sam Dillon, D.J.'s father, liked the area. So did his wife. They settled there and D.J. was born in Timbergold County. D.J.'s mother had been killed in an auto accident a few years ago and Dad Dillon had remarried.

Mrs. Keene frowned. "Caleb, if I didn't have my life's savings invested in that old mansion, I'd just walk away and forget the whole thing!"

"*What?*" Grandpa sputtered as though he'd tasted a mouthful of vinegar by mistake. "You'd keep me from having more fun than I've had in many a year! I'm a'going to sneak up on that there ghost and *catch* him!"

D.J. laughed. "How are you going to do that, Grandpa?"

"Don't rightly know yet, D.J., but I'm a'going to find a way!"

The boy stood up. He was taller than any boy in his class, though he was as thin as a rake handle. "Grandpa, you're going to need help!"

The old man snorted and peered over the top of his bifocals. "Don't need no help catching something that never was!"

"Just the same, Grandpa, I want to go with you."

"I was a'figuring on you a'taking care of Stranger while I was gone."

D.J. liked Grandpa's dog, but he liked adventure more. "You could get a friend from church to take care of Stranger. Then I could go with you."

Grandpa hesitated as Dad Dillon came through the back door with an armload of oak and madrone* for the wood-burning stove. "What's this about you going somewhere, D.J.?"

"I want to go with Grandpa and help him—uh—investigate the problems Mrs. Keene is having with the house she bought at Devil's Law."

Dad Dillon was a powerfully-built man who loved physical things. Even splitting firewood was a pleasure for him. He tossed the armload of wood into a large metal-lined box in the corner.

"Remember what we discussed when Christmas vacation started, D.J.? You're not going *anywhere* until you get your history paper written."

"Ah, Dad!"

"You had all semester to get that paper done! Now you've got to get it finished before school starts again the first week in January, or you're liable to flunk. Isn't that right, Mrs. Keene?"

"Well, Mr. Dillon, the state *does* mandate that a student be proficient in certain basic subjects, including California history. While D.J. is a very good student, he's been derelict in not completing a required essay."

Dad nodded. "And that's serious, right?"

"Well, D.J. does face the possibility of being held back a year and not graduating with his class this spring unless—"

Dad interrupted again. "That settles it, D.J.! You're not going anywhere until you write that paper!"

"But I don't even have any ideas! How can I write about something when I don't have anything to write about?"

Dad removed his heavy leather gloves. "You can think about that while we're driving your grandfather to the bus."

Mrs. Keene exclaimed, "Bus? I thought you'd drive Caleb down to the mansion."

"Planned to, but I got a couple of late orders for firewood that have got to be delivered. So he'll just have to take the bus."

"Oh, Caleb! I'm sorry! It's such an imposition! If I could only see well enough to drive anymore—"

Grandpa stopped Mrs. Keene with a chuckle. "I've ridden that bus many a time, Ouida! Besides, I can sneak up on that there ghost because he won't know I'm a'coming."

"Oh, I couldn't let you do that, Caleb! I'll phone ahead and have Miss Harridan meet you at the bus depot."

D.J. recognized the name of the housekeeper who had been living at the mansion since before Mrs. Keene bought it.

"No you don't, Ouida! Nary a word to anybody! I'm a'going to catch that there ghost—or whatever it is—my way! That means nobody knows I'm a'coming! Absolutely *nobody!* Now, you all can visit a spell whilst I pack. Then we can ride into Stoney Ridge together."

D.J. was both sad and excited as he rode into town with his father, his teacher, and his grandfather. D.J. wanted to help chase that "ghost" more than anything—especially more than writing a history essay.

But Dad Dillon had spoken, and that was that. So they put Grandpa on the bus and took Mrs. Keene to her small, neat house. Then D.J. and his father went home.

That night D.J. unsuccessfully tried to come up with an idea for his history paper, but his mind wouldn't stay on the subject. He wanted to share Grandpa's adventures. At least, D.J. wanted to talk about the ghost to his best friend, Alfred Milford, but Alfred didn't have a telephone. D.J. went to bed without writing one line on his essay.

He awoke the next morning to hear Dad's voice down the hallway. He was obviously talking on the telephone.

"Give that to me again, Mrs. Keene," Dad said.

D.J. could tell by his father's tone that something was wrong. He slid out of bed, grabbed his robe, and hurried down the hall to the kitchen.

Dad was just hanging up the phone. "That was your teacher," he began.

D.J. nodded, sensing something was wrong.

"She was just talking to the housekeeper at the mansion."

"And?" D.J. prompted, feeling his fears rise.

"Your grandfather didn't arrive there."

"What do you mean, Dad?"

Dad said quietly, "He never showed up. He's disappeared!"

Chapter Two

THE MYSTERY DEEPENS

D.J. felt his heart slide right down to his bare feet. He loved Grandpa in a special way. Then D.J. brightened. "Oh, I know why!" he said. "He told Mrs. Keene that he didn't want anybody to know he was coming, so Grandpa must be nosing around without anybody knowing he's there!"

Dad Dillon took a slow, deep breath while considering the possibility that D.J. was right. Sam Dillon's immense chest seemed out of proportion to his stocky body. His legs were short, but everything about him was powerful from a lifetime of hard, outdoor work.

"That sounds like your grandfather, all right, D.J. He always did have a mind of his own. Well, let's hope you're right."

D.J.'s stepmother came in from the back porch where the boy could hear she'd started the washing machine. "Who was on the phone, Sam?" she asked.

Her short blond hair had already been brushed quickly. She was slightly plump with a nervous habit of letting her hands flutter when she talked. It had been hard for D.J. to get used to the idea of Dad being married to anyone besides Mom, who was buried in the cemetery near the school in town. D.J. called the former Widow Higgins "Two Mom." He had been unable to call her Mother or Mom because that's what he had called his own late mother. But Dad's new wife was D.J.'s Mom too, so he called her Two Mom as a satisfactory compromise.

"Mrs. Keene just called about my father," Dad replied. He walked to the kitchen range and lifted the lid on the stainless steel pot of oatmeal bubbling there.

Two Mom asked, "What about him?"

Dad glanced at D.J. and then explained about Grandpa's trip.

Two Mom placed the wooden spoon on the range top and turned to look up at her husband.

"I don't like it, Sam! Since there are no such things as ghosts, that means somebody's up to something no good. It could be dangerous."

"Now, Hannah! Don't go getting yourself upset! My father's all right. In a few days he'll be home bragging about how he chased this ghost thing and scared it so bad it left town."

Dad grinned at his own humor, but D.J. wasn't so sure.

"Two Mom could be right," he said. "Whoever's behind the ghost thing must have a good reason, and that might be strong enough to make him dangerous to anybody who's poking around."

Dad scowled. "Is that why you wanted to go with your grandfather? To get yourself in danger and worry Hannah and me half to death?"

D.J. gulped. He hadn't meant to do anything that would keep him from still going to Devil's Law.

Two Mom poured a cup of coffee and handed it to her husband. "I still don't like it! Something mighty strange has been going on at that place ever since Mrs. Keene bought it and started fixing it up.

"That probably means somebody doesn't want her to have the place, and they're trying to scare her off. Or ruin her. I mean, what with sinking her life savings into restoring the place and all."

Nine-year-old Priscilla came yawning from the hallway. She was a grumpy person when she first got up. Her brown hair was always wild, but this morning it was a total disaster from not having yet been combed.

"What's going on?" she asked in a grouchy voice. "You're all talking so loud you woke me up." She dropped sleepily into one of the upholstered plastic breakfast chairs by the formica-topped table.

Priscilla was D.J.'s stepsister. Her father, Two Mom's first husband, had been killed in a logging accident some time before D.J.'s own mother died. Two Mom and Dad had been married less than a year.

D.J. explained quickly about Grandpa and the ghost. He got a cup from the pegs on the wall by the range. He poured himself some hot chocolate and sat down at his regular place across from his stepsister.

Her brown eyes widened with interest. "If it's not a ghost, and Grandpa catches whatever it is, then what?"

"Catches *whoever* is more likely the way it is," Dad said, sipping his coffee. "But I don't think my father's going to do anything more than poke around so he can look good in Mrs. Keene's eyes. Sometimes I think he's kinda stuck on her."

"Why Sam!" Two Mom exclaimed. "They're just two old childhood friends."

D.J. looked at his father with sudden curiosity. "Grandpa's just trying to help her out," he said.

"I just wish you'd made him promise to phone us when he arrived," Two Mom said. "Well, everyone wash up for breakfast so D.J. can start studying."

An hour later, bundled up in boots, heavy winter jacket, and new green and red Christmas stocking cap, D.J. climbed the steep steps to Alfred Milford's house. It had taken some talking to convince Dad and Two Mom to let D.J. leave home without working on his history composition.

The boy had persuaded them by explaining how Alfred would be able to help him study at the library. Alfred was a year younger and a grade behind, but he was so smart the other kids called him "The Brain." Alfred seemed to know about everything, or he knew how to look it up.

The door opened at the top of the stairs and Alfred came out while D.J. was only halfway up.

The two friends grinned at each other and called greetings. D.J. was tall and thin, but Alfred was downright skinny. He looked like a scarecrow in a heavy winter coat too big and too long for him. He had an owlish look from wearing heavy glasses thick as the bottom of a soda pop bottle.

He wore a Russian style cap with ear flaps turned

down. His scuffed boots, which were too big, clumped clumsily as he hurried down the wooden stairs.

"I was just going to the little store to call you, D.J.," Alfred said, giving his friend a friendly punch on the right shoulder. "Let's take the dogs and go exploring."

D.J. took a deep breath. "Can't." He explained about his problem.

Alfred groaned, unconsciously using his gloved right thumb to push his glasses higher up on his nose. "Want to study here or at the library?"

"You got any good books on California history?"

"Some. Picked them up at garage sales, mostly, for a dime. Are you looking for anything special?"

"Do you know anything about Devil's Law?"

"That's across the river in Nugget County. I've been there and read up on it. But I don't have much on it in my books. We'd better go to the library. Wait till I tell my mom."

A short time later the boys were hurrying through the clear, crisp December morning toward Stoney Ridge's tiny branch library. D.J. explained all about Mrs. Keene's problems with the "ghost," and Grandpa's taking the bus to check out the situation.

"Wow!" Alfred cried, picking up a handful of snow from a vacant lot they were cutting across. "Couldn't we have fun catching whoever's behind all that ghost business?"

"Sure could!" D.J. agreed. He watched his friend mold the snowball and toss it at an old tin can glistening in the melting snow of the vacant lot.

"Hey!" Alfred cried, his face lighting up with an

idea. "If you got your composition written fast, do you think maybe your folks would let you go over to the mansion? We've still got five days left before Christmas vacation ends!"

D.J. thought about that, feeling his boots sliding a little on the frozen trail across the lot. "Be worth a try. But there's so much research to do before I can write—"

"I already know some things about Devil's Law," Alfred interrupted. "I'll tell you, and you write them down in your own way. While you're doing that, I'll look up references and things because Mrs. Keene always wants a bibliography."*

The boys reached the high concrete sidewalk by the small branch library just as an old mud-splattered sedan nosed up next to the curb.

D.J. said, "That's Brother Paul's car."

Paul Stagg was the lay pastor of Stoney Ridge's only church. Both boys liked the big man, and hurried to meet him. All the car windows had been covered with frost during the night. Small areas had been scraped clean so the driver could see. But the car's heater apparently wasn't working, for the windows had steamed over.

Through the windshield, smeared where the wipers had barely removed the snow and road grime, D.J. could see Brother Paul's face.

He was 6'4", but looked 7 feet tall in his usual saddle-colored cowboy boots and a high-peaked 10-gallon Stetson.* When he slid out of the car to the pavement, D.J. saw the man had on an old sheepskin working cowboy's coat and faded blue jeans.

"Hi, Brother Paul," the boys called together.

The lay pastor's deep bass voice rumbled up from his big chest. "Well, howdy, D.J., Alfred. You're out bright and early on this pretty day."

The right front passenger door opened and Kathy Stagg stepped out. D.J. broke stride at sight of the pastor's daughter. D.J. hadn't seen her through the car's fogged-over windows. She was months younger than D.J., with reddish hair that partially escaped from under a cowgirl's white hat with a wide brim and a flat crown. She wore pale gray leather boots with inch-high heels and topped with a fringe of rabbit fur. The matching blue jeans and jacket made her seem taller and more slender than usual.

" 'Morning, D.J.," she said with a smile. "Alfred, how're you?"

"Fine," Alfred replied, but D.J. didn't say anything.

"We're going to Devil's Law," Kathy announced, pulling new leather gloves over her long, slender fingers.

"That's right, boys!" Brother Paul reached out a huge hand and engulfed D.J.'s in a powerful handshake. "Too nice a day to stay home, and my wife has a church committee meeting, so Kathy and I are going down to play tourist. Want to come along?"

Brother Paul finished shaking hands with Alfred. He clapped his gloved hands together. "Would we! That'd be fantastic! Only . . . " his voice dropped and he glanced at D.J.

"Only what?" Kathy prompted.

Briefly, D.J. explained about his problem.

"Well," Brother Paul said when D.J. had finished,

"as soon as I cash a check at the mercantile store, Kathy and I'll be on our way. Sorry you boys can't come along."

"Me too," D.J. said. He turned toward the library which had once been a retail store. "Oh, Brother Paul, would you keep an eye out for my grandpa while you're there? Give us a call tonight if you see him. OK?"

The lay pastor promised to do that, then led his daughter a couple doors down to the town's only grocery store.

Alfred approached the library door. "You should have told them about the ghost, D.J."

D.J. didn't answer. He was thinking about Grandpa Dillon, and wondering if something really had happened to him.

D.J. didn't recognize the older woman behind the counter. She was probably from the main library at Indian Springs. She was just hanging up the telephone when the boys walked in.

"Oh," she said, peering over the top of half-glasses, "I just had a phone call about two boys. Are either of you D.J. Dillon?"

"I am."

"Your father just phoned to say you should call home right away."

Chapter Three

THE SEARCH AT DEVIL'S LAW

D.J. felt his heart jump. He turned to Alfred. "Dad hates talking on a telephone, so it's got to be about Grandpa! Something's happened to him!"

"Maybe not!" his friend answered. He glanced at the librarian. "Did Mr. Dillon say why he wanted D.J. to call home?"

The woman read the boys' concern as she shook her head. "No, he didn't. Here, we're not supposed to do this—but you can use our phone."

D.J. also disliked using a telephone, but he barely thought of that as he reached for the receiver.

He dialed with shaking fingers. Dad answered on the first ring.

"Hi, Dad. It's D.J."

Dad didn't waste any time. "How long will it take you to finish your research for that history paper you've got to write?"

"A couple of hours or so. Alfred and I just got here

to the library. Why? Any word about Grandpa?"

Sam Dillon always used a low monotone when he talked on the phone. "Not a word. But I was wondering if you could get enough studying done so that you could write your essay before the end of the week?"

D.J.'s heart speeded up. "I can do it," he said with controlled excitement. "Any special reason?"

"I thought maybe you might like to drive over to Devil's Law with me and sort of look around for your grandfather this afternoon."

Dad's voice was low and very controlled, but D.J. sensed his father's inner concern.

"I'll be ready when you say, Dad."

"Good. I'll have Hannah pack a sandwich for you. So I'll pick you up about noon at the library."

D.J. kept his voice calm too. "OK. Oh, Dad—I thought you had to help Alfred's father deliver some firewood today."

"I'm going to run by John Milford's right away and see if he can't handle those deliveries by himself."

D.J. swallowed hard. So Dad was really worried about Grandpa!

The boy kept his voice calm. "Dad, would you ask Mr. Milford if Alfred can go with us?"

"Guess I could. Well, bye, D.J."

The phone clicked dead. D.J. handed the instrument back to the librarian, thanked her absently, and looked at Alfred. Quickly, D.J. explained what his father had said.

Alfred listened thoughtfully and then asked quietly, "Are you thinking what I'm thinking?"

"Yeah! Dad's trying not to scare me, but he's *really*

worried about Grandpa disappearing."

"You'll find him," Alfred said with a smile. "And faster if I can go with you. Why, there's no mystery you and I can't solve together!"

D.J. managed a weak smile. "We never had to solve one with a ghost before." He turned toward the stacks of books in the converted store. "Well, let's try to find all I'll need to write that composition before Dad shows up."

It was hard for D.J. to concentrate on doing research for his history paper. But Alfred came up with an idea.

"Hey—I know what! You can write about Devil's Law!"

D.J. considered that a moment. "That would work," he agreed. "And I could tie in the story about the mansion and the ghost and everything!"

"Great! Mrs. Keene will give you an *A* for sure on that!"

"Good. Let's get started!" D.J. replied.

Within a few minutes D.J.'s mind was focused on the research. Though there weren't many books on the subject in the small branch library, Alfred found enough to keep D.J. busy checking indexes and making notes.

Alfred stood on a small footstool with tiny casters to peer at books on the top shelves. D.J. sat on the library floor with his back against the far wall. His feet stuck out straight on the floor. Books that Alfred had pulled off the shelves were piled on both sides of D.J. He was a fast reader. His blue eyes skimmed the pages.

"Hey, Alfred—listen to this!"

Alfred turned around and peered down. "What?"

"This book says that most gold camps were really wild and lawless by the mid-1850s, but the forty-niners* claimed that the worst of all had no law except the devil's. So that's how the town got its name of Devil's Law."

"Boy!" Alfred mused. "Can you imagine a place without any law at all?"

"There's more!" D.J. continued, his voice rising. "A San Francisco newspaper published a story from a little girl—"

Alfred interrupted. "I didn't think there were any women and children in the gold camps."

"There weren't many," D.J. replied, tapping the page on his lap. "But there were some. Like this little girl. She wrote a letter to Jesus."

"To Jesus?"

"That's what this book says. I guess somebody sent her letter to the newspaper. Here's what she wrote:

" 'Goodbye Jesus, we're moving to Devil's Law.' "

Both boys smiled at the idea, then D.J. took a deep breath. "That's all very interesting, but we've got to know more about the Chinese laborers so we can know about the one that's supposed to haunt the mansion Mrs. Keene bought."

Alfred said, "Let's try to find out how the ghost story got started."

The boys still hadn't found that material when the front door opened and a blast of cold air shot through the library and into the stacks. D.J. recognized Dad's voice.

"We'll have to finish this later, Alfred. My father's

here!"

Alfred said he'd put the books back on the shelf except those that D.J. wanted to check out. D.J. nodded his thanks and ran to meet his father at the front of the library.

"Anything on Grandpa?"

"Not a word. You ready?"

"What about Alfred? Can he go?"

"His folks said it's OK as long as you two stay together."

"All right!" D.J. exclaimed. He rapidly checked out some books at the desk and eagerly waved his friend forward.

Dad said, "If that's your last book, D.J., let's roll."

D.J. quickly told Alfred the good news that he could ride with the Dillons. The boys stepped outside the library and started for the family sedan parked beside the curb. They were greeted by the loudest bark imaginable.

"Hero!" D.J. cried. "Dad, you brought my dog!"

"And Mrs. Keene," Sam Dillon replied.

The boys approached the sedan. Mrs. Keene was sitting in the front passenger's seat. She rolled her window down and called a greeting to the boys.

"Your father was kind enough to invite me to come along, D.J.," she said. "I thought if you were going to have to ride with your teacher, you might also like to have your dog."

Dad grinned and opened the front door to slide under the steering wheel. "Mrs. Keene and I figured Hero can't do any harm, and he might help us pick up Grandpa's trail. OK, you two get in the backseat with Hero and buckle up."

D.J. threw his books on the floor of the backseat and hugged his little mutt. Hero was about as ugly a dog as anybody could imagine, but he was also so full of love for D.J. that nothing else mattered.

"We'll find Grandpa, won't we, Hero?" D.J. asked, as the mongrel flopped down on the boy's lap and rolled over sideways to have his chest rubbed.

Hero was half-hound, a quarter Airedale, and the rest Australian shepherd. He had the longest nose D.J. had ever seen on a dog. It stuck out from his muzzle like a giant black olive, well beyond his powerful jaws. Hero was shaggy-haired, reddish-brown and stub-tailed. He was scarred from many a fight with a bear because he was a "hair-puller."* D.J. had originally gotten Hero to chase Ol' Satchelfoot,* an outlaw bear.

As the car headed down from the mountains toward the foothills of Nugget County, Dad handed a brown paper sack of sandwiches across the back of the front seat.

Alfred immediately took a cheese and baloney (as everyone called it), but D.J. asked the question uppermost in his mind.

"Dad, where're we going to start looking for Grandpa?"

Dad didn't reply, and D.J. had an uneasy feeling start in the pit of his stomach.

Mrs. Keene replied, "We've already looked in Timbergold County."

D.J. exclaimed in surprise, "You have? *Where?*"

"We called the sheriff's office."

"The sheriff's office?" D.J. interrupted in alarm.

"It seemed like the logical thing to do, D.J.," Mrs. Keene explained. "They checked the hospitals, the sheriff's and highway patrol offices—"

"Why?" D.J. cried in alarm.

"Just in case," Sam Dillon answered grimly. "They can do it better and faster than we could."

D.J. had to swallow hard before asking the next question. "What . . . what did they say?"

Dad didn't answer. Mrs. Keene glanced at him and then turned to look over the backseat at the boys. "They've had no accident reports for the last few days. No hospital admittances of anyone answering Caleb's description. Your father plans to do the same thing in Nugget County."

D.J. swallowed hard, fearful of what might have happened to Grandpa Dillon.

Mrs. Keene changed the subject. "What'd you boys study this morning?"

D.J. explained, then added: "But we couldn't find anything about how the ghost story got started at your mansion."

The teacher chuckled and turned to look at the boys. "That happened because mostly Chinese and Irish laborers worked on the transcontinental railroad. It was finished in 1869. The next time you head up Interstate 80 toward Reno, look high up on the mountainsides and you'll see the snowsheds that were built over the rails so the trains could go through in the winter. It's the same railroad completed after the Civil War."

D.J. nodded. "I've seen them. They look like long wooden tunnels covered with snow."

Alfred finished his sandwich and asked, "What's that got to do with the ghost?"

Mrs. Keene explained. "Chinese and Irish workers

were imported to work on the railroad. The Chinese had a contract that said that if they were killed or died here, their bones had to be shipped back to China. That's why there are no Chinese graves in the Mother Lode cemeteries."

"Hey!" D.J. exclaimed. "Come to think of it, Alfred and I have explored lots of those old graveyards but we've never seen one Chinese name."

"That's right!" Alfred agreed. "We've seen headstones with Jewish, Irish, Italian, Mexican, English, and other names—but never a Chinese!"

Mrs. Keene continued. "Legend has it that one of the Chinese railroad workers was killed and his body secretly buried in a hidden grave. Of course, his remains could not be shipped back to China."

"And," D.J. guessed, "when some of those pioneers imagined or heard strange sounds, they decided it was the Chinese man's ghost!"

"That's essentially correct, D.J. Actually, however, the story didn't get much attention until a rich timber baron built a mansion over the grave site. At least, that's what most people at the time decided had happened."

"Your mansion?" Alfred asked.

The teacher nodded. "The story was that the Chinese man's ghost thought his bones would never be found, so he started prowling the mansion—moaning and groaning."

"So that's how it came to be called 'the moaning mansion'?"

Mrs. Keene nodded.

Alfred shook his head. "Even if the man *was* dead and buried, his soul would have gone to God."

D.J. protested, "It's just a legend, Alfred!"

"Unfortunately," Mrs. Keene continued, "sometimes intelligent people begin to believe in such things. Fear of the unknown, I guess."

Dad asked, "Then why'd you buy the place?"

"Of course, I don't believe a word of the story, Mr. Dillon. Besides, there hadn't been any reported activity of the so-called ghost for many years."

"Until right after you bought it, huh?" Sam Dillon guessed.

"That's true," the teacher said. "But we skipped an earlier part. What makes the mansion so ideal for a modern bed and breakfast place is the rich lore of other events connected with the place."

"Such as?" D.J. prompted.

Mrs. Keene said, "The timber baron who built the place didn't live long. So a colonel bought the mansion. He didn't believe in the ghost, of course, and that's what started all the real trouble."

"A colonel?"

"Well, everyone called him that. He was a Southern sympathizer before the Civil War. After the war was over and President Lincoln had freed the slaves, the colonel supposedly still kept slaves at the mansion. Hid them in an old limestone cave or tunnel under the mansion."

Alfred's eyes widened. "Is there really something like that under the mansion, Mrs. Keene?"

She chuckled. "So the story goes, Alfred."

D.J. mused, "I remember from fourth-grade California history that this state was admitted to the Union as a 'free' state, and slavery was *never* legal here."

"That's true, D.J. But there are historical cases of slaves being kept in California. In fact, there was a great deal of anti-Lincoln feeling here, especially in Nugget County."

Dad cleared his throat. "Devil's Law is just ahead."

The teacher nodded. "So it is!"

Both D.J. and Alfred had been to Devil's Law before. Begun in 1849 when gold had been discovered in the nearby Grizzly River, Devil's Law was considered a "ghost town." It now had less than 500 residents who mostly catered to tourists.

The residents lived in very old frame houses built after the last great fires that destroyed other Mother Lode towns. The main street was lined with red adobe* buildings having heavy iron shutters. That had been a way the miners tried to keep fires from destroying everything.

D.J. glanced out the window, hoping he'd see Grandpa, or maybe Kathy Stagg and her father walking along the high, irregular concrete walks. But there wasn't a familiar person anywhere. When the car was parked, the two boys and two adults got out and walked up and down the narrow streets looking for Grandpa in various stores and side streets. Hero followed D.J. Dad showed Grandpa's picture to several small store owners, but they didn't recognize him.

Next, Dad stopped at the sheriff's office, the highway patrol office, and even at the tiny bus station. Nobody remembered seeing anyone answering Grandpa Dillon's description.

Sam Dillon drove the car slowly down the main

street of Devil's Law in a final hope they'd see the old man. But at the top of the hill leading out of town, D.J. sighed deeply with great sadness.

The boy cried, "He couldn't have just disappeared! He couldn't have!"

Mrs. Keene said softly, "There's one other place we could look—the mansion."

Sam Dillon mused, "But you said you'd checked with the people there and they hadn't seen him."

"It's only a suggestion, Mr. Dillon."

Dad nodded. "Then let's do it!" He stepped down on the accelerator and the sedan picked up speed, heading out of town.

D.J. leaned forward to rest his chin on the back of the front seat between Dad and Mrs. Keene. "Boy! I can hardly wait to see the place!"

"You'll see it in a minute when we cross the river and start to climb out of the canyon. It'll be off to your right. Well, actually, you'll see the cemetery on No Hope Hill. The mansion's just beyond."

D.J. and Alfred turned the direction Mrs. Keene pointed. The sedan rounded the curve. D.J. glanced at the top of the great mountain rising above the river.

"There it is!"

It was the spookiest house D.J. had ever seen. He shivered, but not from the cold. He had a funny feeling that something terrible was about to happen.

Chapter Four

THE WARNING

"It's huge!" Alfred cried. "Three stories tall and it covers the whole top of the hill!"

"That's called 'No Hope Hill,' Alfred," Mrs. Keene explained. "It got its name because miners said there was no hope of finding gold there. So the pioneers started the cemetery up there because the land was useless. The mansion was built across the street much later."

"I wouldn't want a house across from a creepy old graveyard!" D.J. said solemnly. "Especially one as spooky as that house!"

The teacher chuckled. "Though it hasn't had a coat of paint in a decade or more, underneath that peeling and flaking is genuine redwood. That house will last for another century or more with the good care I plan to give it."

D.J. asked, "What do they call that style of building, Mrs. Keene?"

"Actually, D.J., it's a combination of architectural styles popular around here in the old days. The roof line, rear corner tower, and the detailing on most of the exterior are what's called 'Queen Anne.' But the hoods over the windows are called 'Stick,' and the roof fret* work and the front tower are called 'Second Empire.' "

D.J. had heard of Queen Anne buildings because there were lots of them in the Mother Lode. But he'd never heard those other names. He stared at the rear corner tower.

Mrs. Keene seemed to read his mind. "That one is called a 'Witches Hat.' Looks to me more like an ice cream cone turned upside down."

"Too scary for ice cream," Alfred said. "How big is this old house, anyway?"

"Fourteen bedrooms, plus many other rooms. I'll give all of you a tour as soon as you've met Miss Harridan and all the others who live here."

There was something exciting about being able to explore a spooky old place like this in the daytime, D.J. thought. But he would not want to do it at night.

Sam Dillon's car topped the hill, passing the cemetery on the left and an open pasture on the right. There wasn't another house within sight. A barbed wire fence separated the mansion from the empty pasture. Dad pulled up to an immense iron gate. Through it, D.J. could see a long, curving gravel driveway winding through live oak* and valley oaks* toward the mansion.

"The gate's unlocked, Mr. Dillon," the teacher said.

D.J. jumped out to open it. His fast movements

alarmed a mixed flock of domestic gray geese and guinea fowl.* The honking and shrill, rocking cries could have been heard for half a mile.

D.J.'s eyes skimmed the mansion and the large open yard around it. There were lots of dense shrubs and long-established trees. He recognized evergreens like cedars,* ponderosas,* and digger pines* mixed with winter-bare liquidambar,* red and sugar maple trees.* At this lower elevation, there were no familiar sugar pines* and no snow.

D.J. pushed against the heavy wrought iron gates. They opened at the middle, swinging away and inside on protesting rusty hinges. When Dad had driven through, D.J. closed the gate and jumped back into the car.

He put his hands over his ears. "Those birds sure are noisy!"

Mrs. Keene explained, "Geese and guinea fowl make the best watchdogs in the world! Nothing can get by them!"

"Better than dogs?" D.J. asked.

"At least in the daytime when they can see," the teacher said. "Look! Here comes everybody from the house."

D.J. saw a tall, slender woman in a black dress and white apron leading three men onto the nearest porch. They stopped on the edge of the driveway and waited.

"That's my housekeeper, Miss Harridan," the teacher said. "The man behind her is a real estate salesman, Mr. Hatchett. The short, stocky young man is our handyman, B.B. Shorqwat. The older, bald man is Mr. Grabnot. They were here as roomers and boarders before I bought the place."

As Dad stopped the car in front of the high-stepped porch with its ornamented posts. D.J. glanced beyond the house to the barn. "Hey! There's someone else in uniform! Just going into the barn!"

"That's Sheriff Cadwaller," Mrs. Keene explained.

D.J. thought about his grandfather and jumped out of the car as soon as it had completely stopped. He turned to Hero in the backseat and commanded, "Stay!"

Mrs. Keene introduced everyone to the housekeeper. Miss Harridan greeted each visitor warmly.

"D.J.?" she said, reaching out to shake his hand. "You're one of Mrs. Keene's students, I presume?" When the boy nodded, the housekeeper turned to Alfred. "And you're Alfred? I imagine Mrs. Keene is very proud to have such nice-looking boys in her class!"

D.J. thought Miss Harridan was a little gushy, but she seemed sincere. The boy turned to look at the three men as his teacher introduced them.

"This is Mr. Hatchett. He sells real estate. Sam's father is the one who disappeared on his way to this mansion. That's who Sheriff Cadwaller is looking for out by the barn."

Hatchett reached out and shook Dad's hand. "Hope they find him soon, Mr. Dillon."

"Thanks. Call me Sam."

He shook hands with each of the other two men as Mrs. Keene presented them, but none of the three men offered to shake with D.J. or Alfred.

Hatchett merely nodded to each of the kids.

The handyman, B.B. Shorqwat, who looked like he might once have been a professional football lineman, barely bobbed his head in acknowledgment of the introductions.

Only the older, bald man seemed friendly. "Glad to meet you all," he said with a quick smile. "I'm sorry about your missing relative. Well, if you'll excuse us, we'll get back to what we were doing."

The three boarders retreated up the high steps and into the mansion. Mrs. Keene suggested showing her visitors around the grounds. She led the way toward the back of the mansion. D.J. fell in step beside his best friend to whisper.

"Not very friendly, were they, Alfred?"

"Brrr!" Alfred whispered back. "Except for the housekeeper and that bald man, they sure didn't make us welcome. Wonder why?"

"Good question!" D.J. answered as the teacher rounded the corner of the house and raised her voice slightly.

"That's the barn back there, of course. Nothing in it anymore. There's a woodshed behind it, old chicken houses off to the right—no chickens anymore—and a former harness shed is now used as a garage. You boys may want to explore later. First, we'll tour the inside of the mansion."

As they started to turn back, the uniformed officer walked out of the barn door and approached the group. He was a very skinny man, quite tall, wearing a khaki uniform and a quilted jacket zippered shut against the cold. A revolver rode at his left hip. The man had big bags under his eyes and the skin under his chin was so loose it wattled. He reminded

D.J. of a mournful-looking bloodhound.

The housekeeper introduced him as Sheriff Cadwaller.

"Sam Dillon?" the officer said, shaking hands with Dad. "You must be the relative who filed the missing persons report on Caleb Dillon."

"Yes—he's my father. D.J.'s grandfather," Sam Dillon replied.

"The sheriff in Timbergold County asked me to keep an eye out for the old gentleman—so with the permission of Miss Harridan here, I've been looking around."

D.J. exclaimed, "Did you find him?"

The sheriff's big brown eyes looked out from his sad-looking face. "Sorry, not a sign. Well, now, don't look so downhearted, D.J.! I have ascertained from the bus driver in Devil's Law that Mr. Dillon *did* get off there. But there's only one taxi in town, with one driver, and he didn't remember driving anyone out here that day."

Miss Harridan asked, "Could he have hitch-hiked?"

Dad shook his head and D.J. agreed. Grandpa wasn't a hitchhiker.

The sheriff continued. "There's no evidence that he got this far. So maybe he wandered off somewhere when he got off the bus. No offense, but old people sometimes do get a little absentminded."

D.J. spoke sharply. "There's *nothing* wrong with Grandpa's mind!"

"I didn't say there was," the sheriff replied mildly. "It's rare—but sometimes people get amnesia. Often older people just get confused and wander off on their own. We usually find them in a couple days."

Sam Dillon said softly, "He's not like that. That's why I'm afraid maybe something bad has happened to him."

"Well, Mr. Dillon, we don't have a lot of crime in this county. I don't think he's in any danger. I've got to get back to town. I'll keep looking and keep you posted."

D.J. watched the officer walk to a four-wheel-drive station wagon he'd parked behind the garage. He waved to them as he drove toward the gate.

D.J. thought Mrs. Keene was trying to ease the tension when she asked, "Miss Harridan, would you mind fixing hot drinks while I give our guests a quick tour of the mansion's interior?"

"I was just going to suggest the same thing. It's cold out here. Coffee and hot chocolate fine with everyone?"

The inside of the house was dark, cold, and spooky. D.J. immediately caught a whiff of a smell he couldn't quite place.

Alfred sniffed and whispered, "Smells like bacon. And dust!"

D.J. inhaled deeply, following the two women. "Yeah! That's what it is, all right! Bacon and dust! Not just musty, like most old houses smell."

Mrs. Keene explained that she was going to paint everything a lighter color, install brighter lights and electric wall heaters in every room. She had already installed them in each second floor bedroom. Almost every room in the house was kept closed off in the winter since the wood-burning kitchen stove and the stove in the living room couldn't really heat the whole house.

D.J. was glad he still had on his coat as his teacher led the way through a maze of rooms on the ground floor. Each had 12-foot-high ceilings. All of the rooms were larger than in any house D.J. had ever seen. The formal dining room and great living room held massive dark pieces of furniture. Mrs. Keene explained that the tables, chairs, china cabinets, and high boys* were all handmade antiques and at least a hundred years old.

The living room was fairly warm because it was heated by a big wood-burning stove. Every wall held photographs of older, full-bearded men and sad-looking women with high collars. Their hair was parted in the middle and pulled down severely on both sides of their heads. D.J. thought that not one of those pictured people could have been happy.

"Which one's the colonel who lived here during the Civil War?" D.J. asked.

"I don't know," the teacher replied. "None of these pictures is named or dated. However, I *do* recognize that steel etching of General Robert E. Lee in profile."

The boys stopped to look at the Civil War general. Both agreed they wouldn't have recognized him from the side view.

The tour moved from the warm living room down a cold, dark hallway to the foot of the staircase in the middle of the first floor. As D.J. followed the others up the steep, curving steps, he ran his hands along the smooth, dark mahogany banisters. There was a landing at the top with a wall phone. There were long, wide hallways on both the right and left sides of the stairs.

Mrs. Keene explained. "There are eight bedrooms on this floor and six on the third." She pointed to more stairs going up to the third floor, but they were blocked by a chain. "There's dry rot and other problems on the third floor, so it's not safe to go up there yet. Besides, Miss Harridan hasn't finished with rewiring it. I'll just give you a quick peek on this second floor."

Alfred asked, "Did Miss Harridan really do all the rewiring?"

Mrs. Keene smiled. "Oh, yes! She's very handy in lots of ways around the house."

D.J. and Alfred exchanged grins, then turned their attention back to Mrs. Keene.

The teacher said there were four bedrooms to the left. D.J. could see two doors on both sides of the dark hallway lit by a single small overhead bulb. Mrs. Keene said the three boarders lived in that wing with one room on the far end kept locked as a storage area.

"Down this way," Mrs. Keene added, leading the way to the right, "we've got four more bedrooms. Miss Harridan has the first one on the right. The other three are ready for occupancy. If you children were going to stay overnight, these would be yours."

Mrs. Keene opened three doors, flipping on bright modern lighting fixtures that looked old-fashioned to keep the period atmosphere of the mansion. D.J. took a quick look, noticing that the closed-off rooms were cold. The second on the right had closets larger than the Dillon bathroom at home. The farthest bedroom across the hall had what she called an armoire.* She explained it was a movable cupboard or wardrobe with shelves and doors where clothes could be hung.

Every room had heavy gilt picture frames, mostly rounded and ornately carved, hung from wires suspended from a small railing about two feet below the ceilings. Instead of pictures of people, as downstairs, all the second floor paintings were pastoral* scenes of waterfalls, pastures with horses, and flower gardens.

Mrs. Keene closed the last door and started back down the dark hallway toward the landing. "I've already invested heavily in restoring the mansion, as you can see from these rooms. When I finish with the third floor, we'll have the largest bed and breakfast inn throughout the Mother Lode."

She paused, then turned to look quickly at her guests. "That is, if I don't lose it. But I'd gladly trade what I've got invested in this place just to know Caleb is safe."

D.J. wished the teacher had shown them what was inside the two towers seen outside the house. D.J. asked, "What's inside the towers?"

Mrs. Keene frowned. "I'm not really sure. Miss Harridan says it's not safe up there, so I've never looked. I think she said there was some old junk such as you'd find in an attic."

D.J. was still curious. "How do you get up inside the towers?"

Mrs. Keene paused at the top of the stairs. "You'd have to ask Miss Harridan. But don't go near the towers! You might get hurt. Well, let's go back downstairs."

As the boys trailed the adults starting down the stairs, D.J. whispered to Alfred, "I'd like to take a look in all the other empty rooms, especially that locked one on the far end of the boarders' wing, and on the third floor."

"You think your grandfather's up there?" Alfred whispered, turning to look upward. "I don't think so! It's too cold!"

"Maybe there's a portable electric heater up there?"

"You heard what Mrs. Keene said—the wiring is not safe."

D.J. nodded and raised his voice with another idea. "Mrs. Keene, is it true that the colonel who owned this place kept slaves even after the Civil War?"

The teacher paused on the stairway and looked back up. "That's one of the stories handed down from the past. But I've never seen anything more exciting around here than a small cellar."

"Cellar?" D.J. echoed. "Could Alfred and I see it?"

"Not right now. It's under the kitchen and was used to keep things cool before refrigeration. Well, let's get out of these cold hallways and have our hot drinks in the kitchen where it's warm."

D.J. was restless and anxious to find Grandpa. When he entered the kitchen, he asked, "Mrs. Keene, would it be all right if Alfred and I go exploring some more?"

"Why, I suppose so, if it's agreeable with your father."

Sam Dillon nodded, so the boys quickly drank their hot chocolate and walked out toward the barn.

Alfred glanced back at the great bulk of the old mansion. "Gives me the creeps!" he exclaimed. "Like it had a secret or something."

"Yeah," D.J. agreed. "I wonder why those three men who live here weren't more friendly a while ago?"

"Maybe they've got secrets too."

"All three of them?"

The friends were passing an immense old cedar tree with a trunk at least three feet wide.

"Hey, boys!"

The voice was low, almost a hiss. D.J. and Alfred stopped suddenly and glanced toward the tree. It was so big they couldn't see anything except a man's brown shoe sticking up from an exposed root on the far side of the trunk.

"Don't look this way!" The voice was a hoarse whisper now. "Look toward the barn or something!"

The boys automatically obeyed. D.J. started to ask, "Who are you?" but the voice cut him off.

"Take it from a friend—it's not safe around here."

"Wh . . . what?" D.J. asked, involuntarily looking at the big tree. He caught a glimpse of the man's face as he jerked back behind the big trunk.

The voice was stronger, more urgent. "You heard me! Go on to the barn or someplace as though nothing had happened, then get back to the house and leave! Don't ever tell anyone about this, and don't ever come back! It's not healthy around here!"

"Now just a minute!" D.J. exclaimed. "We're guests of Mrs. Keene! She's our teacher and she owns this place! We can go anywhere we want!"

"Yeah!" Alfred chimed in. "We don't have to leave until we're good and ready."

The man's voice came once more. "You've been warned! Get out of here while you can!"

Chapter Five

A CLUE TO GRANDPA'S DISAPPEARANCE

The friends tried to walk casually toward the barn, but D.J.'s heart was racing with excitement. "I recognized him! It's Hatchett, the real estate man!"

Alfred gave a low whistle. "Why did he do that?"

"I don't know, unless maybe he's seen Grandpa."

"Then why wouldn't he have told us that instead of trying to scare us off?"

"I don't have any idea."

"Well, his warning sure scared me! I'm ready to get out of here!"

"Me too, in a way," D.J. agreed. "But it also makes me *sure* Grandpa's around here somewhere! If only we could find a clue!"

Alfred asked, "Are you going to tell your father what Mr. Hatchett said?"

"Soon's I can. Well, here's the barn. Let's take a look inside—casual like—and then get back to the house. I want to talk to Dad privately. There's no need of scaring everybody who lives here."

The boys paused outside the sliding wooden door into the red barn. Their eyes automatically checked the tracks in the dust between the concrete walkway and the door.

"No dog," Alfred said. "No cats."

"No pets," D.J. agreed. "But what kind of a track is *that?*"

Both boys bent to examine where D.J. was pointing.

"Looks sort of like a pig's hoof, or a deer's," Alfred mused. "Only it's not all there. Only half. Maybe a crippled animal?"

D.J. knew animal tracks the way he knew the letters of the alphabet. He shook his head and got down on his knees to put his face close to the strange track.

"Not an animal," D.J. announced, still studying the impression. "Man-made. See how rounded it is? Sort of like half of a—HEY!"

D.J. leaped to his feet. Alfred jumped back in surprise.

"What's the matter, D.J.?"

"I know what that is!"

"What? Tell me!"

"It was made by my grandpa's Irish shillelagh!"

"What?"

"Alfred, he's been here! Grandpa's *been* here, I tell you!"

D.J. left Alfred by the tracks to keep anyone from accidentally erasing them while D.J. went to get his father. In the excitement about finding the track, D.J. forgot to tell Dad Dillon about the real estate man's warning. Instead, the boy excitedly recalled when Grandpa decided to chase the ghost for Mrs. Keene. Grandpa's cane slipped on the floor of his home, and he almost fell.

D.J. concluded, "Dad, that's when Grandpa showed me the rubber tip of his Irish shillelagh had cracked. He was going to get it replaced. But I'm sure this track here was made by that split-end on his cane!"

Sam Dillon bent to examine the track both boys pointed out. Slowly, Dad stood up and shook his head.

"You're an awfully good tracker, D.J., but with just one track—"

"I tell you, Grandpa's been here, but the people denied it! Why? Because they're lying—that's why! They've got Grandpa hidden someplace!"

"Or at least one of them has," Alfred added. "Did you tell your father about the warning?"

"Warning?" Dad asked with concern. "What warning?"

"I forgot to tell you," D.J. replied lamely. He quickly reported about the man behind the cedar tree.

"You're sure it was Hatchett?" Dad asked, gazing toward the house.

"I'm sure," D.J. replied.

Dad was thoughtful a moment. "Well, we'd better not take any chances. Let's clear out. Then I'll come back and talk to that Hatchett myself."

"He warned us not to tell *anybody*, Dad!"

"I'm going to do what I've got to do, D.J.!"

"Ah, Dad! Nothing's going to happen while it's still light, with all of us here! So why can't Alfred and I look around some more before we leave?"

"Yeah!" Alfred cried. "Maybe we can find some sign of that old tunnel or cave or whatever it was where the colonel kept slaves after the Civil War! Maybe that's where Grandpa Dillon's being kept."

Dad's voice was tinged with annoyance. "That's all just tall tale stuff, boys! Your imaginations are running away with you! There's probably no such thing as a tunnel or cave, and never was."

"Could we look around—huh, Dad? If we stay in sight so you can see us every second?"

Dad nodded slowly. "You come when I honk the car horn! And stay in sight *every* second! You hear me?"

The boys agreed and continued their explorations. They started with the barn because it was closest. They slid the heavy door open enough to squeeze through the opening, but still stay where Mr. Dillon could see them. The great structure was empty and gloomy. There wasn't even any hay. Pigeons exploded from the high loft, startling the boys. The birds flapped noisily in alarm through the top opening where the hayfork still hung, unused for years.

The huge building was lit only by weak winter sunbeams squeezing through cracks and knotholes in the western side. In the gloom, D.J. could make out some parts of old farm machinery. Dusty license plates were nailed to the wall.

"No place to hide in there," Alfred said as the boys stepped back into the yard and slid the big barn door shut.

"Let's try the chicken house, the garage, the hen house, and any other buildings we can find," D.J. suggested.

Those searches also yielded nothing, leading the boys to one logical conclusion. If Grandpa was here, he was somewhere in—or under—the mansion. There was no way the boys could explore that by themselves.

"Too bad we can't stay overnight," D.J. observed as he led the way toward the bluff overlooking the river. "Then we could explore the third floor and the cellar."

"If there is a secret tunnel or anything, it'll probably have a hidden entrance," Alfred said.

D.J. wasn't sure if that was logical or just something his friend's imagination had created. As D.J. thought about it, the boys came to the top of the bluff. The river was a silver ribbon far below.

Alfred kicked a boot heel on the top of the bluff. "This is almost straight down. Could they have dug a tunnel in this bank, like gold miners sank shafts*?"

D.J. turned to look at the mansion. "I suppose a tunnel could run from here to under the house. The hard rock miners did a lot of things harder than that. Hey, what'd you say we get Hero and let him nose around? See if he can pick up Grandpa's scent?"

"Hero's a bear dog," Alfred protested. "He's not trained to trail people like a bloodhound!"

"I know, but it won't hurt to give him a little run anyway."

The little hair-pulling bear dog was so glad to be freed from the car that he almost twisted himself in two with joy. D.J. snapped the leash into place and let Hero out. He began jumping up in the air, bouncing off D.J.'s knees and almost knocking him down.

"Easy, Hero!" D.J. warned. "You're supposed to be on my side!"

The boys casually walked back to the barn. D.J. pulled the dog up to the barn door. For a moment, D.J. didn't think Hero was going to do anything, then he stopped dead still.

His long, funny nose dropped into the dust. His short tail began twisting like a short propeller gone wild. Hero barked once—a single, sharp, joyful sound.

"He found it!" D.J. cried. "I told you that Grandpa's been here!"

After the one bark, the dog lifted his muzzle and sniffed toward the river. He whined and strained against the leash.

D.J. had mixed feelings. "Well, now we know for sure that Grandpa was right here. But did he walk away—or did someone carry him?"

Alfred touched his friend's arm comfortingly. "Now don't go getting upset! We'll find him!"

"Yeah," D.J. agreed. "Hey! Look at Hero! Do you think he smells Grandpa? After all, a cut-across* dog does that when he's trailing a bear. I mean, he smells the quarry in the air instead of in the dust like a trail hound."

"We could see where he'd go," Alfred suggested.

D.J. nodded and extended his arm full length, allowing the leash to fall slack. "OK, Hero—go! Go!"

In a few minutes, the boys had followed the little mutt back to the top of the bluff overlooking the river. The dog whined and wanted to go down the steep bank, but D.J. held him in check.

"We can't go down there or we'll be out of Dad's sight."

"Maybe we don't need to," Alfred said excitedly.

He knelt and pointed in some sand off to the boys' right. "There're more of those funny cane tracks! And a man's footprint."

D.J. bent to examine the new find. "No doubt about it, Alfred. That's Grandpa's footprint! And there're a few more cane prints! Now we know Grandpa was here for sure! We've got to find him!"

"But how?" Alfred asked, straightening up.

"We need to find a way to stay overnight! Then we can look around without anyone watching us!"

The boys started back toward the mansion. They were still discussing their find as they passed the barn. Suddenly, Hero gave a low growl and walked stiff-legged toward the sliding barn door.

"Easy, Hero!" D.J. called, tightening his grip on the leash. "What's the matter—huh, boy?"

D.J. slid the barn door open slightly. Hero surged eagerly through the opening, leaping to the end of his leash. The boys stayed in the open doorway and peered into the gloomy interior, their eyes adjusting to the semidarkness.

Hero's wild jumps showed the direction they should look. D.J. saw the door slide open on the other end of the barn and a man's figure slip through.

"Did you see who it was?" Alfred asked anxiously.

"Yeah! It was the handyman—Shorqwat! Alfred, he was spying on us! Do you suppose he heard what we said as we walked by this barn?"

"Hard to say," Alfred admitted. "But why would he spy on us? Unless he and that man who warned us are together in this mess with Grandpa's disappearance."

D.J. calmed Hero down and left the barn door

open to step back into the barnyard again.

Suddenly, the distant alarm cries of geese and guinea fowls reached the boys.

"There's a car coming down the road," D.J. said, pointing. "Looks like Brother Paul's!"

D.J. remembered that the lay preacher and his daughter had planned to "play tourist" at Devil's Law. They'd probably decided to drive out to the mansion since Mrs. Keene was a member of Stoney Ridge's church where Brother Paul pastored.

Alfred caught his breath. "Hey! He's sure driving funny! He's weaving all over the road!"

The friends stared as the distant vehicle straightened out a moment, then cut in sharply toward the mansion's iron gate.

"He's going to hit it!" Alfred exclaimed.

At the same instant, the car braked suddenly and barely nudged the twelve-by-twelve post. The iron gate shuddered.

Kathy jumped out of the car, her cowboy hat trailing on a string behind her flying reddish hair. She shoved hard at the gate. It opened slightly and she pushed through, then started running hard toward the mansion.

"Something's wrong!" D.J. cried. "Come on, Alfred! Something terrible's happened!"

Chapter Six

A SECOND WARNING

By the time D.J. and Alfred reached the front gate, Kathy had led Sam Dillon and the other adults on a dead run back to Brother Paul's car. Two of the boarders helped Dad ease the big lay preacher out of the driver's seat and onto the gravel driveway in front of the gate. He didn't seem to be totally unconscious, but he was obviously very hurt or sick.

The boys and Hero came panting up to the scene in time to hear Kathy explaining in a high, frightened voice.

"We had lunch and started to drive out here to see Mrs. Keene, and Daddy began to feel sick to his stomach. Then just a little way back, he suddenly got terribly sick! He barely got the car stopped before. . . . " Her voice broke.

D.J. saw that Brother Paul's eyes were open, but they looked strange. His cowboy shirt was soiled, and his whole color was terrible. His reddish hair was plastered wetly against his forehead with perspiration. Absently, the boy picked up the big man's Stetson as Dad finished checking him over.

The teacher turned to Kathy. "Lunch! Did you both eat the same thing for lunch?"

"Why, yes—no! Well, we ate at a restaurant, but right afterward Dad got something from one of those street vendors with the little pushcarts. He said he was still hungry, so he bought a sandwich from a street vendor, but I didn't have anything. Why? What's wrong?"

D.J. saw Dad and Mrs. Keene exchange glances. She said something softly to Dad, who nodded.

"He may have food poisoning," the teacher said. "Miss Harridan, will you phone for an ambulance?"

"No!" Dad spoke sharply. "I'll drive him to the emergency room! Much faster! Men, help me push his car out of the way so I can get through the gate! D.J., see if Brother Paul's coat is in his car!"

D.J. said a silent prayer for the preacher as the three men from the mansion shoved Brother Paul's car out of the way. D.J. ran alongside the car and pulled the door open.

"Yip! Yip! Yip!" A tiny dog's thin, high bark made D.J. jump in surprise. The Staggs didn't own a dog.

"Hey!" D.J. yelled as a small Yorkshire terrier shot out of the backseat and onto the ground. Instantly, Hero was upon the tiny, hairy morsel.

"No, Hero! *No!*" D.J.'s sharp commands broke his dog's forward rush.

The Yorky didn't stop. He charged up to the bigger Hero and barked wild challenges. Hero disdainfully turned a solidly muscled shoulder to the pup.

D.J. didn't have time to see more. He found Brother Paul's coat and turned to see Dad running to his own car. In a moment, Dad brought it to a screeching stop beside the man. In moments, the four men had gently folded Brother Paul's big body into the backseat and placed his jacket over him.

Kathy wanted to ride with Dad, but he shook his head. "No offense, but you're too worked up. I need a cool head with me. Only room for one."

"I'll go," Mrs. Keene said. She hurried around the front of Dad's car. "Miss Harridan, please make everyone comfortable, won't you?"

"Of course," the housekeeper replied.

Kathy's freckles stood out starkly against her usually pinkish skin. "I can't just stay here and wait!"

D.J. gently touched her arm. "It'll be OK!"

Dad called, "We'll call as soon as we know anything!" In a moment, the car was out of sight.

"Well," Miss Harridan said gently, "now all we can do is wait."

"And pray," D.J. said softly.

He hadn't known an afternoon to be so long since he'd waited in the emergency room at Indian Springs after his mother was in the accident that took her life. The boy tried not to think that the same thing could happen to the big preacher.

Miss Harridan suggested they all go to the large living room. B.B. Shorqwat, the handyman, added wood to the big stove and then left the room without looking at the boys.

"Oh!" Kathy exclaimed, jumping up from a Duncan Phyfe* chair. "My dog! I almost forgot!"

D.J. looked up in surprise from an old-fashioned sofa where he and Alfred had sat down. He'd forgotten about the little Yorkshire terrier that was still outside with Hero.

"Your dog?" D.J. asked.

Kathy nodded. "We drove by the Nugget County pound today and I saw this little guy in a pen all by himself. I fell in love with him. Since the pound would have put him to sleep, Dad let me get him. Miss Harrington, may I bring him in the house?"

"Harridan," the housekeeper corrected with a smile. "Yes, of course, Kathy. Well, if you boys will excuse me, I've got to attend to something in the kitchen. There's no television, but make yourselves comfortable. There are some books on the shelves."

Alfred went to the long, darkly colored bookshelf in the corner. D.J. wandered around the room. He absently reexamined the metal etching of General Robert E. Lee in profile, and then the various somber men and women who stared from the past through old photographs. There were no pictures of children.

D.J. really wasn't seeing the pictures, however. His mind was on all that had been happening.

D.J.'s thoughts were interrupted by Kathy hurrying in from outside, her flat cowboy hat hanging down her back by a string around her throat. She carried the terrier in her arms. D.J. saw that the dog's long, silky straight coat was almost steel blue from tail to skull, but his legs, chest, and head were tan.

"Isn't he cute?" Kathy asked, shaking her reddish hair in characteristic fashion.

"I named him Smooch," she said, sitting down in the chair again. "You can see why. He's always kissing me like this!"

"Smooch?" D.J. cried in mock disgust. "What kind of a name is that for a dog?"

"It's a good name!" Kathy said soothingly, holding the dog up in her arms in front of her face. "Isn't it, Smooch?"

"Yuk!" Alfred whispered. "That's not kissing! That's licking—plain old licking! All over her face!"

"Maybe he's tasting Kathy before biting her," D.J. replied softly with a grin to his best friend.

"He's doing no such thing!" Kathy replied, making kissing noises toward the dog held in front of her face. "That's smooching, dog style!"

Alfred whispered, "I may be sick."

D.J. thought it was good that something was keeping her mind off her father's health. But the moment he thought about it, Kathy's face changed as though she was thinking about it too. She put the dog down on her lap as Miss Harridan entered with a tray.

"I thought all of you might like some hot chocolate," the housekeeper explained.

Kathy gently pushed the Yorky onto the floor and stood up. "Uh . . . would it be all right if I called the hospital first, please?"

"I'll do it for you, Dear. Here, would you pass the tray to the boys? I'll bring the phone."

D.J. half expected to see an old-fashioned wall phone, but the housekeeper reached inside a tiny wall cupboard by another overstuffed chair. She withdrew a modern handset and dialed.

In a moment, she hung up and reported. "There's no news except that the doctor is with your father.

We'll try again in half an hour or so. They've called your mother, Kathy. She knows where you are, with all of us."

The kids had finished their beverages when Miss Harridan picked up the phone and called the hospital again. She hung up and smiled.

"I talked to the doctor himself this time. He's finished treating Mr. Stagg, who is now being monitored. I assume that means they're watching him. But he's going to be all right and we'll soon hear from Mrs. Keene or Mr. Dillon."

Miss Harridan was right. Almost at once, Mrs. Keene called, asking for Kathy. D.J. watched anxiously as she slid the phone up to her ear.

He read the good news in her face before she spoke. "He's going to be all right! Thank God!"

D.J. and Alfred let out joyful yells. Then Kathy handed D.J. the phone. "Mrs. Keene wants to speak to you."

The boy was surprised. He pressed the receiver to his ear and said hello.

"D.J., don't say anything—just listen!"

Mrs. Keene's words were low but intense. "We don't want to alarm Kathy, but Brother Paul is still very ill. Your father and I are going to stay here at the hospital overnight. We've called your stepmother, Mrs. Stagg, and Alfred's parents."

D.J. listened in silence as his teacher continued. "Keep Kathy's spirits up. Tell Miss Harridan that we can't come back for you children tonight. She'll provide dinner and beds. We'll get back to you in the morning—or sooner, if it's necessary. Are you afraid?"

"No, Mrs. Keene."

"That's fine! Your father told me about the warning you got from Mr. Hatchett. Mr. Dillon is reluctant to leave you children there, but he and I are confident nothing will happen with so many of you there."

D.J. swallowed hard. He didn't feel so sure, especially since he hadn't told Dad about Mr. Shorqwat spying on them from the barn.

The teacher's voice concluded in D.J.'s ear. "I can't tell you how sorry I am to have gotten all of you into this situation! But there's one thing I want you to remember—if you hear strange sounds in the night, somebody is causing them. There are no ghosts, of course. Tomorrow, I'm sure we'll find your grandfather. Well, goodnight, D.J." The phone clicked dead.

D.J. managed a reassuring smile at everyone. "Dad can't come back for us tonight. We're going to get to stay here tonight! Won't that be great?"

Kathy didn't seem at all sure, but Alfred echoed D.J.'s opinion. "Maybe we'll get to see the ghost!"

"*Ghost?*" Kathy cried in alarm, glancing around. Then she grinned. "Oh, no! You boys can't scare me or Smooch! He'll protect me!"

The boys laughed. D.J. told the housekeeper what Mrs. Keene had said about supper and beds. Miss Harridan seemed delighted. She led the way up the winding stairway and down a long hall with closed doors on both sides.

"Kathy, this'll be your room," the housekeeper said, opening the third door on the right.

D.J.'s eyes skimmed the high-ceiled room and the

huge four-poster bed with massive headboard and lacy white canopy.

Kathy swung around, smiling broadly. "Oh, it's beautiful! Smooch and I love it, Miss Harridan!"

"Glad you like it. Snap the electric wall heater on. It'll be comfortable in a few minutes. Now, boys—let's go on down past my room to yours. There are no phones in any of the rooms, of course, but there is one at the top of the stairs."

"We won't need one," D.J. said as the housekeeper opened the door to the boys' room. The minute he said it, he wasn't sure that was the truth.

D.J. glimpsed a room larger than Kathy's, with two very high four-poster beds near the side walls. A massive highboy separated the beds. A large window with Priscilla* curtains framed the highboy. There was an armoire for the boys' coats. The side walls were decorated with heavy, old-fashioned hanging picture frames, except these were hunting scenes of upland birds. There was a bathroom with shower and tub too.

"I hope you'll be comfortable here, boys," Miss Harridan said.

"We'll be fine," D.J. said, hoisting himself up to the top of the bed and bouncing to test it. He had never seen a bed so high. His feet were at least two feet from the dusty rose carpet.

"Perhaps you boys would like to freshen up for dinner? Turn your heater on now. I'll take Kathy down with me to help in the kitchen."

When the boys were alone, Alfred went into the bathroom to wash up. D.J. looked around the bedroom. For some reason he couldn't explain, he began to feel very uneasy.

He thought about Brother Paul, and Grandpa being missing but maybe even close by. And spending the night in this place, knowing they'd been warned to get away. As Alfred came out of the bathroom, D.J. explained his feelings.

His friend said, "I thought you wanted to spend the night here."

"I did—when it was daylight and the idea seemed like fun. Now it's downright scary."

"It's your imagination, D.J. That's the trouble with writers—you're always thinking wild thoughts."

D.J. planned to be an author someday. He gave Alfred a friendly punch on the shoulder and went into the bathroom to wash up. "I've got to look for Grandpa, so we need to borrow a flashlight to go exploring tonight when everyone's asleep."

Alfred protested, "I'm not sure that's such a good idea, D.J. I mean, without your father or Mrs. Keene here."

D.J. tried to shake off his concerns. "It'll be OK! As soon as I dry my face, let's go down to supper."

As Alfred swung the door inward, D.J. saw an envelope. It had been placed against the outside of the hallway door.

"What's that?" Alfred asked.

D.J. picked it up. "Nothing on the outside. But I guess it's for us." It wasn't sealed, so he opened it.

Alfred said, "Read it out loud."

D.J. swallowed hard before reading the large block print letters.

IF YOU DON'T GET OUT
OF HERE BEFORE BEDTIME,
YOU'LL END UP LIKE
THE OLD MAN.

Chapter Seven

WHEN THE GHOST WALKS

The boys stepped inside their room, closed the door, and discussed the situation. Neither had heard anyone outside in the hallway before the note was found. Miss Harridan had taken Kathy downstairs, so that meant the housekeeper hadn't put the note there. That left the three men boarders as suspects.

D.J. glanced again at the unsigned note. Was it from Hatchett, who'd warned them out by the barn? Could it be from B.B. Shorqwat, who'd been spying on them from the barn? Maybe this second warning was from Mr. Grabnot. D.J. shook his head as the thoughts spun through it. Even if the boys wanted to leave, they couldn't possibly get away tonight.

D.J. reviewed the possibilities. "If we call Dad at the hospital, he'd have to leave Mrs. Keene and Brother Paul at a time when they might need him. If someone from here would give us a ride, it'd only be as far as Devil's Law. We'd all end up at the hospital waiting room."

"At least it'd be safe," Alfred mused.

D.J. shook his head. "Whoever kidnapped Grandpa doesn't want two or three more people to disappear; especially kids. The whole county would turn out and they'd go over every inch of this place.

"No, Alfred, I'm convinced that somebody's just trying to scare us off. I don't think we're in any real danger."

"Wish I could feel as confident," Alfred replied.

D.J. concluded, "Besides, I'm convinced Grandpa's being held against his will someplace close. If we stay, we can look for him and maybe rescue him tonight."

"If we don't disappear or run into that—that ghost—or whatever it is."

"That's part of the scare tactics," D.J. said emphatically. "Whoever's behind this whole thing—and for whatever reason—is trying to frighten us away!"

"Your grandfather disappearing is *more* than a scare, D.J. Remember what the note said."

"Well, I'm in favor of staying the night," D.J. concluded. "Now, let's go down to supper—and act natural."

"Oh, sure!" Alfred scoffed. "Sit there with somebody who's kidnapped your grandfather, warned us not to stay here, and act natural!"

The mansion's formal dining room had a long table graced by a cloth of Irish linen, flanked by high-backed oak chairs with a crystal chandelier hanging over the center. There was a sideboard* and a leaded glass china chest that reached to within a couple of feet of the 12-foot-high ceiling.

D.J. had to take a deep breath and force himself to smile as he glanced around the table. Miss Harridan sat at the head of the table nearest the kitchen. Kathy sat on her left with Alfred next to her and D.J. last.

There was a vacant chair at the far end. Across from D.J. the real estate man picked up his napkin. The bald man was directly across from Alfred, while the husky handyman was opposite Kathy.

Which one had kidnapped Grandpa and written the note to the boys? Were they all in on it? D.J.'s thoughts raced as he watched to see if anyone would say grace. Miss Harridan didn't seem to notice. She picked up a soup tureen and started it around the table.

D.J. lowered his head and said a silent blessing, remembering Grandpa and Brother Paul at the same time. He raised his head in time to see Kathy and Alfred had done the same thing.

As dishes were passed family style, D.J. spoke to the man across from him. Mr. Hatchett had hidden behind the cedar and warned the boys to leave.

"How's the real estate business these days?"

The man's eyes were gray and cold, without warmth. "I've seen worse—I've seen better." He dipped his spoon into the soup.

D.J. tried the second man. "You're Mr. Grabnot, aren't you?"

"That's right. Sylvester Grabnot." The bald man didn't look at the boy. "I'm mostly retired. Used to be in the promotion business." The way he said it seemed to indicate that was the end of the conversation as far as he was concerned.

D.J. tried again. He turned to Shorqwat, whom the boys had seen running from the barn that afternoon.

"Did you ever play football, Mr. Shorqwat?"

D.J. received only a hard look but no reply from the third man.

Mr. Grabnot spoke disapprovingly. "You don't follow football, do you, kid?"

D.J. didn't like being called "kid." "I don't see much football on TV," he admitted.

The bald man nodded. "Then you don't know that B.B. Shorqwat was one of the greatest tackles that ever played the game."

D.J. was embarrassed. Alfred came to his rescue.

"D.J. and I do a lot of exploring and things; we don't stay home much on Saturdays."

Shorqwat grunted. "I was a professional! I played on Sundays."

Kathy said brightly, "Oh, that explains it! We all go to church on Sunday!"

The three men looked at the visitors as though that was such an unlikely thing that they couldn't believe it was true.

D.J. squirmed uneasily, then tried again. "What does a promotion man do, Mr. Grabnot?"

For a moment, D.J. didn't think the bald man was going to answer. Finally he said, "I helped people get their products or services better known."

D.J. needed information if he was to find Grandpa. The boy turned toward the end of the table. "Miss Harridan, were you always a housekeeper?"

The woman laughed lightly and flashed her easy smile. "I started out in Hollywood as a radio actress."

"Radio actress?" D.J. echoed.

"Before television, there were dramas—stories—on radio. I played a few bit parts."

Kathy asked, "What was it like?"

"Radio was fantastic! Nothing but music and sound, yet for years we created a thousand worlds through the theater of the mind! Then television came along, and. . . ."

Her voice trailed off. D.J. glanced at Miss Harridan. Her smile was gone. For a second, D.J. saw a strange, hard look in her eyes. Then she smiled again.

"But life goes on, and we adjust," Miss Harridan said.

Alfred finished buttering a slice of bread. "How'd all of you come to live here, in this old mansion?"

Miss Harridan explained. "When I got tired of the rat race in Hollywood, I started looking around for a nice, quiet place. I found this one and got a job from the real estate company that managed it as one of its properties."

The real estate man shrugged when D.J. looked at him. "I work for another real estate firm that's trying to buy this place for a client."

D.J. blinked. "But Mrs. Keene just bought it a year or so ago. She's going to retire here and have a bed and breakfast place! She won't sell it!"

Mr. Hatchett smiled thinly. "Everything's for sale if the price is right."

D.J. thought about that but Kathy spoke across the table. "And you, Mr. Shorqwat? What brought you here?"

"Nothing special. When I got too old to play the game, I just started drifting. I only knew how to play football. But I'm good with my hands, so the management company hired me to help fix up this place."

"And," D.J. guessed, "when Mrs. Keene bought the place, she kept you on?"

The conversation flowed more easily as the meal went on. Still, D.J. had an uneasy feeling that the men were all being careful to watch what they said.

D.J. would have liked to have a handwriting sample from the people who lived at the mansion to compare with the note he'd gotten, but that was impossible. Frustrated, he lapsed into silence and let others talk. There was very little of that. D.J. sensed an uneasy tension that was so thick, "you could have cut it with a knife," as Grandpa Dillon would have said.

After dinner, the men excused themselves and went upstairs. The boys volunteered to take Hero and Smooch outdoors because Kathy was afraid of going outside. She helped Miss Harridan with the dishes while D.J. and Alfred bundled up. They borrowed a two-cell flashlight, and took both dogs out.

Smooch only stayed a couple of minutes and then wanted back in the house. The boys turned the little terrier over to Kathy and took Hero for a longer walk. This gave the boys a chance to talk and scout around outside.

There was a full moon and a clear sky, but the shadows were deep and threatening. D.J. kept Hero on a tight leash as the boys circled the mansion.

"What're we looking for, D.J.?"

"I don't really know. A light in a third story window, or under the house. A place where a secret door might be. Any place that Grandpa could be held prisoner."

The boys watched Hero for any reaction to somebody in the night, but the little dog frisked about playfully. D.J.'s light probed every bush and shadow, but there was nothing unusual at all.

Reluctantly, the boys at last turned toward the barn to chain Hero out of the cold for the night.

D.J. was discouraged, yet hopeful in another way. Grandpa had to be somewhere in or under the mansion, and the entrance had to be inside, somewhere. When everyone was asleep, the boys would try to find that entrance.

As they walked toward the barn's dark hulk, the boys reviewed the supper conversations and drew some conclusions.

D.J. observed, "Miss Harridan gets to stay on as housekeeper, so there's no motive for her to create a ghost story, kidnap Grandpa, or threaten us. Mr. Hatchett, the real estate man, admits he has someone who'd buy this place. So he might be trying to scare Mrs. Keene into selling through the ghost thing."

Alfred continued, "But he warned us to get away. Maybe he also wrote the note; maybe not. Anyway, the bald man, Mr. Grabnot, might make some money promoting the place. Maybe make it famous, like the Winchester House* in San Jose. But that's no reason to kidnap your grandpa or threaten us."

D.J. added, "Mr. Shorqwat, the former football player, also doesn't have a motive we know about."

"So," Alfred concluded, "nobody seems to have a motive except the real estate man. But why would he warn us? That'd make him an even better suspect."

"Shorqwat is also a suspect. Remember he was spying on us from the barn."

"I'm getting a headache from thinking so hard," Alfred said.

The boys slid the barn door open, tied Hero inside out of the night wind, and closed the door. As the friends turned back toward the house, D.J. stopped so suddenly Alfred bumped into him from behind.

"Alfred, look!"

A light was moving across the yard near the mansion. It swung like a man carrying a lantern.

"Who is it, D.J.?"

"I can't see anybody. But notice the light!"

"It's not a flashlight," Alfred whispered. "More like a lantern. Funny shape, though. Not very bright, either."

D.J. asked softly, "A Chinese lantern, maybe?"

Alfred forced a small, weak laugh. "Don't try to scare me, D.J. It's just one of the guys from the house out fooling—"

His voice broke off. D.J. saw the light stop and slowly rise in the air. It floated straight up past the first floor to the near tower balcony on the second floor.

"*That's impossible!*" Alfred whispered.

D.J. saw the lamp stop. By its pale yellow light, D.J. glimpsed a wide Chinese coolie straw hat with the brim turned down all around. Under that, D.J. saw an Oriental face.

Alfred whispered, "D.J., do you see . . . ?"

Suddenly, the lamp went out. The image was gone. D.J. snapped the flashlight on the spot.

Nothing was there!

Chapter Eight

A SURPRISE ON THE THIRD FLOOR

The boys raced into the kitchen where Miss Harridan and Kathy were just putting the last dishes away.

"My! You boys look as though you'd seen a ghost! What happened?" the housekeeper asked, drying her hands.

"Miss Harridan," D.J. asked breathlessly, "how do we get up to the front tower balcony?"

"Why, just go past the boarders' bedrooms to the end of the hall. There's a door—"

"Thanks!" D.J. called, not waiting for her to finish. "Come on, Alfred!"

Kathy called after the boys for an explanation, but they didn't answer her. D.J. led the way up the stairs and down the hallway. He found the door at the end, unlocked the bolt, and flashed the light into the tower room.

It was filled with cobwebs, old trunks, and pieces of furniture. Everything was covered with dust.

"Nobody's been in this room for years," Alfred said softly.

"But we *saw* somebody!" D.J.'s borrowed flashlight touched every article and rested on the door leading to the balcony. "Come on," he said, advancing into the room.

The wooden floor cracked like ice breaking on a pond so D.J. hesitated and drew back uncertainly. He lowered the light to watch as he tested the flooring with a cautious step forward. Satisfied, he took three steps across the room, unbolted the outside door, and flashed his light onto the tiny balcony.

"Nothing! But we both saw that face right here! We saw the lantern, and the hat, and even his face—didn't we, Alfred?"

"We saw *something*," Alfred admitted quietly. "But I'm not sure it was . . . a . . . a person."

D.J. turned around to face his friend. "Don't tell me you're beginning to believe in ghosts?"

"I know what I saw, and now there's nothing there. See? Our footprints are the only things in this dusty place! Come on, D.J., let's get out of here!"

D.J. sighed deeply and led the way back, bolting the two doors. "I just don't understand it, Alfred!"

"Me, neither." Alfred walked beside D.J. down the hallway toward the landing. "What're we going to tell Kathy and Miss Harridan?"

"Just that we wanted to check out this tower room," D.J. replied. "No sense scaring Kathy and maybe having the housekeeper laugh at us."

Kathy seemed a little dubious about the boys'

explanation, but she didn't press the matter.

The housekeeper suggested everyone go to bed early since there was no television and it'd be warmer in the bedrooms. D.J. asked if he could borrow the flashlight overnight, and Miss Harridan consented. She didn't even ask why. She led the kids upstairs.

Kathy went up the stairs with her flat cowboy hat hanging down her neck. She took Smooch into her room and closed the door. The boys went on to their room which was now comfortably warm from the electric wall heater.

Alfred took off his thick glasses, put them on the nightstand, and began undressing.

D.J. asked, "What're you doing?"

"Getting ready for bed, of course!"

"Aren't you going exploring with me when everyone's asleep?" D.J. asked in surprise.

His friend hesitated. "To tell the truth, D.J., I'm kinda scared. I mean, we did see that light go straight up in the air in a way no human could do, and we saw—"

D.J. interrupted. "We saw something that's got a logical explanation, and we're going to find out what it is! Anyway, we've got to look for Grandpa tonight. It's probably the *only* chance we'll get!"

Alfred jumped up and sat on the edge of the high bed. His feet didn't touch the floor. "D.J., would you be mad at me if I . . . I didn't go with you?"

The mountain boy hesitated. "No, of course not. It's just that I'd feel better if you went along."

"And I'd feel better if we both stayed in this room with the door locked! That thing we saw is giving me the willies."

D.J. didn't want to admit it, but he wasn't feeling as brave and confident as he sounded. "Well, I'll make you a deal."

"What?"

"We check out the third floor. If we don't find anything, we'll call it enough for tonight."

"What about the tunnel?"

"I'd like to look for that, but if you don't want to go with me, we'll try that in the morning before Dad comes for us."

"Sounds good to me, D.J. I'll just take off my shoes and crawl under the covers with my clothes on. When you're ready, we can go."

D.J. nodded and opened the armoire to hang up his heavy jacket where Alfred had put his. D.J. saw a couple of old books in one corner of a shelf and pulled them out. They didn't appeal much to him, but they were better than nothing. He removed his shoes and slid under the covers, propped up his head by doubling his pillow, and began to read.

In about an hour the house was totally quiet. D.J. figured everyone had gone to sleep. He put the book on the nightstand and turned to his friend.

D.J. was surprised to hear Alfred snoring lightly. Even with the overhead light on, Alfred slept peacefully. He looked different without his thick glasses.

For a moment, D.J. hesitated. *Should I wake him up? Naw, let him sleep! I'll just take the flashlight and check out that third floor by myself.*

He decided against wearing his heavy boots. They would make too much noise on the third floor. He slipped his heavy coat back on, held his fingers over the flashlight so only a small beam shone, then eased down the hall in his stocking feet.

He stepped over the chain hanging across the bannisters that led to the third floor. Trying to breathe quietly and ease his excited heartbeat, D.J. stepped in the middle of the first stair.

It creaked loudly. D.J. stopped at once, his head cocked to listen. No doors opened. No lights came on. D.J. slid his stocking feet closer to the wall and continued climbing. The stairs did not creak any more.

At the top, breathing a little hard from the steep climb and excitement, the boy grasped the white porcelain knob on the door that blocked his way. Gently, D.J. turned the knob. The door squeaked open.

D.J. stopped, holding his breath. Then he eased the door open just far enough to stick his head around and shove the flashlight past the door.

At first glance, this looked much like the second floor, except there was a large sitting area at the top of the stairs. The high-backed sofas were obviously very old, dusty, and unused.

D.J.'s flashlight probed the darkness in the left hallway. There was a total, eerie silence. When D.J. turned off the flashlight, heavy darkness immediately reclaimed the whole wing.

The hallway to the right was not quite as dark. At the far end, the full moon was shining through a high window. There was a spot of cold light in the middle of the hallway with deep black shadows crouching against the walls. D.J. snapped the light that way. The shadows vanished and old pieces of furniture stood starkly revealed in the wide hallway.

D.J. was surprised to hear himself sigh with relief.

He realized his heart was beating faster than he would have guessed.

I'm not scared, he told himself. Still, he'd be glad when he finished checking out the various rooms.

That didn't take him long. They were cold and bare, except for old pieces of junk and frayed furniture that obviously hadn't been touched for years.

D.J. closed the last door with relief and stood for a moment in the moonlight streaming through the far window at the end of the hallway. He unconsciously snapped off the flashlight and stood looking out the dusty window covered with spiderwebs.

The pioneer cemetery across the street and to the left was clearly visible. The great valley oaks with winter-bare branches cast long shadows across the tumbled tombstones. D.J. could see the rusted wrought iron fences around some graves and untended wild rosebushes that stretched fifteen feet in the air.

It gave the boy a strange feeling. He decided it was time to get back downstairs. He spun around in the moonlight and started to snap his flashlight on again.

That's when he saw the other light.

D.J. automatically sucked in his breath. He forgot his own flashlight as he watched the small beam at the top of the landing.

I'm cut off! It's between me and the stairs!

Then D.J. heard a tapping. It was faint and irregular, but it was so distinct it echoed in the third floor emptiness.

That almost sounds like Grandpa's cane!

D.J. started to snap his light on, then stopped. The second light approached a door D.J. hadn't noticed before. The door opened and closed. The tapping stopped. The lamp was gone.

Barely breathing, the boy flipped his flashlight on and ran on tiptoes of his stocking feet to the door where the second light had vanished.

D.J. swallowed hard, grasped the knob, and pulled the door partially open. He snapped his light up and then drew back in surprise.

He was staring at a blank red brick wall!

A voice behind him demanded, “What’re you doing here?”

Chapter Nine

GHOSTLY FOOTSTEPS

D.J. almost jumped out of his socks! He whirled around, flipping up the flashlight.

"Alfred!"

His friend threw his hands up to shield his eyes. "Hey! You're blinding me!"

D.J.'s heart was in a full gallop and his mouth was suddenly so dry it took him two tries to get his voice to work.

"What's the idea of sneaking up on me like that?" he demanded in a fierce whisper. "You trying to scare me to death?"

"Well, you don't have to get mad about it! I woke up, hearing footsteps up here. I saw your bed was empty and came looking for you! Sorry I fell asleep a while ago, D.J."

"It's OK." D.J.'s heart was slowing down though he could feel adrenalin scalding through his veins. "Did you see it?"

"See *what?*" Alfred adjusted his thick glasses on his nose and pulled his jacket tighter about his thin shoulders.

"The light! The light! It went right through this door and vanished." D.J. flipped his flashlight around on the red brick wall.

"What're you talking about, D.J.? There's nothing there except a wall."

Wordlessly, D.J. closed the door and then opened it again.

"Wow!" Alfred whispered. "Why on earth would anyone build a wall behind a door?"

D.J. didn't have any explanation. His breathing was almost normal and his pulse was about the same. "I thought I heard Grandpa's cane tapping just before I saw the light."

"You did?"

D.J. shrugged. "I'm not sure." He led the way down the stairs, across the chain, and back to the bedroom.

In the lighted comfort of the room, D.J. explained more fully what he had done and seen on the third floor.

Alfred sat on the edge of the high bed, swinging his feet in the air. "You think maybe your grandfather's up there instead of in that tunnel?"

"We don't know that there really is a tunnel," D.J. reminded his friend. "I don't know where the sound came from. Then I saw that light, and when it vanished right into that wall. . . ."

His voice trailed off and he didn't finish his thought. Instead, he said softly, "Alfred, I can't explain any of this. Not logically."

"You mean . . . you're beginning to think maybe there *are* such things as ghosts?" Alfred's voice was tight and thin, as though he was also starting to believe in such things in spite of all he knew.

"I don't know what to think," D.J. admitted.

"What're we going to do now?"

D.J. took a slow, deep breath, battling doubts and fears gnawing at his thoughts like rats against ropes. "I've looked everywhere except under the house to see if we can find a tunnel or cave."

Alfred spoke in alarm. "You said you wouldn't look there tonight!"

"I won't. Besides, I've had enough mysteries and scares for tonight. Let's get some sleep, then look under the house tomorrow before Dad gets here."

"Suits me!" Alfred exclaimed, sliding his jeans off and tossing them on the end of the bed. He swung his legs under the covers and took off his glasses. " 'Night, D.J."

D.J. stripped down to his underclothes and slid under the covers of his bed. He snapped off the light and stared into the semidarkness of the room. The full moon, riding higher in the sky and shining through the window, gave the room a soft glow.

"Lord," D.J. whispered, looking toward the invisible ceiling, "I know there are no such things as ghosts, and yet . . . well, I'm scared! I don't know what to think!

"And where's Grandpa? I hope nothing terrible's happened to him! Take care of him, wherever he is, please. And help me to find him before it's too late."

The boy hesitated, remembered to mention Brother Paul's health, and then added, "Amen."

Feeling a little better, but still very uneasy, D.J. closed his eyes.

It was still dark when he was awakened by something; he wasn't sure what. The moonlight had shifted. The room was still fairly dark. But what had awakened D.J.? A sound? Yes! Footsteps! Coming down the hallway outside the bedroom door.

D.J. sat up to listen better. Whoever it was walked slowly and steadily. Yet the footsteps didn't sound like shoes or boots, D.J. thought. More like something loose on the feet.

D.J. jumped from the high bed to the floor. "Slippers! Chinese slippers! It's the ghost!"

D.J.'s heart was pounding so hard it seemed to be louder than the steps he was straining to hear.

They were closer now . . . closer. D.J. wanted to turn around and shake Alfred awake, but he didn't move.

The steps were closer . . . closer . . . then they stopped! Stopped right outside the door! D.J. turned his eyes to the old porcelain doorknob, reflecting whitely in the shadows beyond the moonbeam's reach. Was the knob turning?

The boy glanced around the moonlit room for some kind of a weapon to defend himself. He didn't see a single useful item except his heavy boots. He bent quickly and snatched one up.

His eyes were snapped back to the door as the next step came.

But it didn't go past the door. Instead it sounded as if it were going right up the outside of the closed door!

"Can't be!" D.J. whispered, staring so hard at the

door that his eyes hurt. But there was no doubt about it. Two more footfalls were heard—each higher up than before!

"Al . . . allll . . ." D.J. tried to whisper his friend's name.

A gentle snore answered him.

The soft footsteps continued up the wall outside the bedroom door. In a moment, D.J. heard them start across the ceiling toward his bed!

No! No! The boy's thoughts exploded as he instinctively drew back. His eyes followed where he heard each clearly audible step, but there was enough moonlight to show there was nothing on the ceiling—yet the steps were coming!

D.J. told himself fiercely, "Maybe I'm hearing someone walking on the floor above! It's not really on this ceiling!"

The footsteps continued, even and unhurried. They passed over the bed and down the wall behind the headboard toward the window.

D.J. couldn't stand it any longer! He swung the boot behind his shoulder, holding it cocked to smash forward while he groped for the light on his nightstand. He snapped it on.

The wall was exactly the same as when he'd turned out the light a few hours ago—except—the footsteps continued! He could pinpoint where each step came from, but there was nothing to be seen except the same pictures in their heavy frames.

D.J. heard the window slide up. He heard it clearly. But with the light on, he could see the window hadn't moved!

The footsteps paused as though someone were

crawling out the window. Then D.J. heard it close with a slight bang. But the pane at which D.J. stared hadn't moved!

The footsteps faded slowly outside the house as though someone were walking down the wall as easily as D.J. would walk on flat ground. Then the footfalls were gone. There was utter, total silence.

D.J. dropped his boot on the floor. Alfred jumped under the overs and opened his eyes slightly. D.J. reached over and shook Alfred's shoulders vigorously. "Hey, wake up! Wake up!"

"Huh?" Alfred's voice was thick with sleep. He turned his face toward D.J.

"Wake up! The ghost was here!" D.J. shook his friend's shoulder again.

"No such thing as ghosts," Alfred muttered sleepily. He folded his arm across his eyes. "Turn off that light, D.J.!"

D.J. started to grab his friend with both hands, then changed his mind. *What's the use?* he thought. *The ghost—or whatever it is—is gone! Wonder if Kathy heard it?*

D.J. crawled back into bed, his mouth again dry as a handful of sawdust, while his heart thudded against his chest as though it were going to burst through. He didn't turn off the light but lay down slowly on top of his bed. He stared at the ceiling.

It was there! he told himself. *I know it's not logical, but I didn't imagine it!*

His thoughts were snapped off and he sat upright again.

He cocked his head to hear better. He thought he'd heard a low moan. He glanced at Alfred. He was breathing evenly, his face visible above the covers.

The moaning sound came again. D.J. slid off the high bed and stood uncertainly in the lighted room, thinking: Kathy? No, it didn't sound like a woman's moan. One of the boarders?

The sound was closer, down the hallway from toward the stairwell. Louder and louder: "Oooohhh!"

D.J. snatched up the flashlight from the nightstand, grabbed his heavy boot from the floor, and leaped for the door. He paused, his ear against it, listening. The moaning was right outside the door!

D.J. reached for the knob and jerked the door open hard!

Chapter Ten

KATHY VANISHES

The hallway was empty! D.J. frantically flipped the flashlight up and down the corridor past the stairwell into the other wing and back again. D.J.'s heart was thumping so loudly he could hear it against his eardrums.

"What was that?"

The voice behind him made D.J. whirl around and start to swing the boot before he stopped.

"Alfred! Stop sneaking up on me like that!" Then D.J. relaxed and asked eagerly, "Did you hear it?"

" 'Course I heard it!" Alfred answered sleepily, adjusting his thick glasses. "But what was it?"

D.J. listened a moment, his head cocked. The moaning was gone. "I don't know." His voice was barely a whisper. "Maybe the ghost of the moaning mansion."

"Don't say that!"

"Well, whatever it was, it's gone—just like the

footsteps."

"Footsteps?" Alfred turned back into the room and closed the door. He pulled the spread off the bed and wrapped it around himself.

D.J. briefly told Alfred about the sound of footsteps that had awakened him, going across the ceiling over his bed and out the window.

Alfred studied D.J.'s face a long time before saying anything. "You're not making that up, are you, D.J.?"

"No, Alfred, I'm sure not!"

"But what's it all mean?"

"I don't know." D.J. didn't want to admit it, but he was having fearful thoughts. He had been wide awake and heard the footsteps. His light had been on when he heard each step going down the far wall and out the window. Those were things no human being could ever do! Then the moaning . . . with nobody there!

"Hey!" he exclaimed aloud. "How come only you and I are standing around here in the middle of the night by ourselves? *Everyone* should have heard that! Especially Kathy. We'd better check on her."

D.J. imitated Alfred, pulling the bedspread off his bed and wrapping it around himself. D.J. took the flashlight and hurried down the hall past Miss Harridan's closed door to Kathy's room.

"Oh! Oh!" D.J. whispered, flashing the light ahead. "Her door's open!"

The boys called softly and knocked on the open door. When there was no answer, they pushed the door open wider. D.J.'s flashlight showed her bed had been slept in, but it was empty.

"Maybe she's in the bathroom," Alfred whispered hopefully.

D.J. reached inside the bedroom and snapped on the wall light. He called toward the open bathroom door.

"Kathy? You in there?"

There was no answer. Still calling softly, the boys advanced and turned on the bathroom light. The shower curtain was pulled back. There were no closets or other places to hide.

"She's gone!" Alfred whispered.

A slight noise behind them made both boys whirl and look under the high bed.

Smooch, the tiny Yorkshire terrier, crouched there, whining softly. D.J. knew instantly that Kathy wouldn't have gone anywhere without the dog—if she'd had a choice. But why hadn't he barked?

The dog refused to come out when the boys called him. Finally, D.J. straightened and stood up.

"He's too scared! Let him stay! We've got to find Kathy!"

"But where'll we look?"

D.J. hesitated. "I don't know, but if she's disappeared like Grandpa. . . ."

"Should we wake up Miss Harridan?"

"I don't see how she could have slept through all that moaning." He moved to the outside of the housekeeper's closed door and listened to determine if she was moving around inside.

Alfred whispered behind D.J., "I don't believe in ghosts! I don't believe—"

"Shh!" D.J. hissed. "It's Kathy we've got to worry about!" He remembered her door had been closed when he and Alfred returned from the third floor. But how long ago had that been?

"What should we do, D.J.?"

He hesitated, still listening outside of Miss Harridan's door. He hadn't heard a thing to indicate she was awake. D.J.'s mind was spinning with countless wild thoughts. He felt sure Kathy wouldn't deliberately have left the room by herself without taking Smooch. The little terrier under the high canopy bed was afraid of something; maybe whatever had taken Kathy—if she had been taken. But why else would she have left her room?

Alfred whispered, "We should have paid attention to those warnings!"

"Too late to think about that!" D.J. said fiercely. "Now we've got to find her!"

"You going to wake the housekeeper?"

"No," D.J. decided, moving back toward the boys' room, followed by Alfred. "We don't know anybody in this house we can trust!"

Alfred closed the door and raised his voice slightly. "But Miss Harridan's never done anything to make us suspicious of her, like the real estate man and that ex-football player."

"We can't take a chance, Alfred! Everyone's a suspect until we know what's going on around here. Now, get dressed and let's go see if we can find that tunnel or cave!"

Alfred's voice was a weak croak. "You mean—go under this old house—now?"

"Right now!" D.J. said firmly, throwing off the bedspread he'd wrapped around himself. He grabbed his clothes from the armoire and dressed quickly. Alfred did the same. D.J. was so scared that his tongue seemed to clack against his dry mouth, but taking action eased the fear.

D.J. decided the logical place to start was the cellar Mrs. Keene had mentioned. Fully dressed including coats, the boys eased down the stairs and into the kitchen. There were two possible doors. The first opened into a cupboard full of food. The second opened onto a flight of wooden stairs going down. The smell of old earth struck D.J.'s nostrils.

With the flashlight, D.J. located an electrical switch. He snapped it on and watched weak light flood the cellar. The boys were careful going down the dozen steps.

It was a small cellar, half the size of the kitchen above it. An adult would have had trouble standing up in the small concrete-walled area.

The concrete was rough finished, clearly showing where two-by-four boards had been used to hold the wet cement until it set. When the board forms had been removed, the walls showed many six-foot-long sections of concrete set end to end. Countless plain wooden shelves lined the walls. A wide assortment of canned fruits and vegetables stretched off in neat rows.

"No doors except the one we came through," D.J. said at last. "No tunnel; no cave. Nothing!"

D.J. sagged against the far end of the cool concrete wall, the familiar odor of a cellar filling his nostrils. "The only other possibility is that the tunnel is in the riverbank and runs back somewhere else under the mansion."

"Unless . . ." Alfred whispered, glancing around the cellar and drawing his jacket tighter about his shoulders, "we're not dealing with . . . a . . . human kidnapper."

"Alfred!" D.J. tried to sound properly shocked. "You don't mean that!"

Alfred lowered his head. "I don't know what I mean! It's spooky! Everything's spooky around here! Seeing the lantern float straight up outside the house, and the Chinese face—plus what you heard going across our bedroom ceiling—"

D.J. had never thought he'd consider that ghosts were real, but he was having fearful doubts. That meant his faith in God was slipping.

"Hey!" Alfred exclaimed, reaching onto a chest-high shelf. "Look what I found!"

D.J. exclaimed, "That's Kathy's flat cowboy hat! She had it hanging down her neck when we all went upstairs tonight!"

Alfred moved closer to D.J. "She's been here tonight!"

"Listen, Alfred," D.J. said, leaning against the concrete wall, "I don't have any idea what's going on, or how it's done, or who's doing it, but . . . oops!"

He felt himself falling as the wall gave way under his weight. He shoved himself away and staggered a couple of steps before falling against Alfred.

"Hey, look at that!" his friend cried, pointing.

The seemingly solid concrete wall had swung slightly inward.

"It's a door!" D.J. exclaimed. A six-foot section had accidentally been pushed open slightly.

He shoved the flashlight through the opening. D.J. remembered hearing that Chinese workers had dug tunnels to store food and items that needed to be kept at a constant cool temperature. D.J. was sure this was such a place.

He and Alfred squeezed through the door and stood just inside the cool, silent shaft. D.J.'s flashlight probed deeper, touching the whitish, rough-hewn walls, ceiling, and floor.

"What do you think, D.J.?"

He turned to face his friend. "Electric wire's been strung along the roof of the tunnel, but I don't see the switch. The flashlight's too weak to let me see the end of the shaft."

D.J. glanced at the flashlight, suddenly aware that the batteries were much weaker than he would have liked.

Alfred stooped suddenly and pointed. "What's that?"

D.J.'s light touched the small object lying on the tunnel floor just inside the concrete door. The boy bent and picked it up.

"Grandpa's rubber tip from his cane! See? It's broken, just as I'd told you before!"

Alfred glanced nervously around. "They're both in here, D.J.! And it's a cinch they didn't find this place by themselves!"

D.J. nodded glumly, flashing the light down the tunnel as far as it would go.

"What . . . what're we going to do?"

D.J. thought quickly. "You go back upstairs and wake everyone up. All of them!"

"But suppose they're all in this together?"

"We've got to take that chance, Alfred! If we awoke one, and it turned out to be the person behind all this, then we'd be in worse trouble! Call the sheriff too!"

"What about you, D.J.?"

"I'm going to try finding Grandpa and Kathy."

"Alone? Down that tunnel?"

"Don't argue, please! Bring the sheriff down here as fast as you can!"

Alfred turned to step through the partially open door, but it began to swing shut.

"D.J.! Look!"

The flashlight had already shown D.J. what was happening. "Quick! Jump through while I hold it open!"

As Alfred leaped to obey, D.J. threw his weight against the door, losing control of the flashlight. It clattered to the limestone floor and went out.

"D.J., I can't get out!"

"I can't stop this door! Jump back here with me before you get crushed!"

Alfred fell backward against D.J. as the door clanged shut. Both boys went down inside the shaft. Total darkness and silence engulfed them!

Chapter Eleven

THE SECRET TUNNEL

For a moment, the boys didn't move. The incredible blackness kept D.J. from seeing his friend. Except for their ragged, frightened breathing, there wasn't a sound in the tunnel.

D.J. reached into the thick darkness. "Alfred?"

"We're trapped, D.J.! Nobody knows where we are, or where Kathy and Grandpa are."

D.J. reached toward his friend's voice and touched Alfred's skinny shoulders. "It'll be OK! Keep control of yourself and help me find the flashlight."

Never had D.J. known such blackness. He felt along the cool floor without success. He could hear Alfred doing the same.

"Here it is!" Alfred's relieved voice came out of the dense darkness. "But it won't work!"

"Let me try!" D.J. reached out and groped until he felt his friend's hands. D.J. took the flashlight and felt it quickly, determining the lens end. He shook it gently and tried the switch. Nothing happened.

"Feel around by the door and see if you can't find a light switch. Maybe it's on a pull string instead of in the wall."

The boys both felt in the darkness. Alfred was making little scared sounds when D.J. felt a string and a small weight touch his hands. He pulled hopefully.

Light flooded the tunnel. D.J. blew out his breath in a big sigh of relief. He glanced up. The overhead electric cords he'd seen earlier also held a series of light bulbs now shining down from wide, white reflectors. He'd overlooked them before.

Both boys glanced down the tunnel to where the line of overhead lights vanished around a curve.

D.J. turned back to the concrete door behind them. "Let's see if we can get out of here!"

The boys leaped to the rough concrete door, but there was no knob; nothing to show how to open it.

"Push along the ends! Feel around!" D.J. suggested, shoving his weight against the markings of the door's outline. "Maybe there's a switch or something!"

Alfred hastened to obey. But in a moment, both boys stepped back, frustrated.

"Must be controlled from somewhere else," D.J. said, panting slightly from his efforts. He turned to look again down the long, cool tunnel to where it made a curve sixty feet or more back.

"Well," D.J. said, holding the useless flashlight as a weapon, "if we can't get out this way, let's see what else we can find."

Alfred groaned but fell into step beside D.J. as they started cautiously down the tunnel toward whatever lay around the curve.

There they peered carefully around the curve, ready to jump back if danger threatened. Instead, they let out sighs of relief. The tunnel opened into a wider room also hollowed out of the limestone. A wall of large concrete bricks stood within the room. There was a large closed door to the left and a window in the wall to the right. It allowed clear visibility into the room.

"What's that?" Alfred whispered.

D.J.'s blue eyes flickered from one object to another. He saw tall banks of electrical equipment with reels turning, transferring tape from one to another. Beside them was a control panel with lots of buttons and gadgets that seemed made to slide up and down.

"I think it's a radio station," D.J. whispered back. "I've never been in one, but I've seen them on television."

"But . . . why?"

D.J. didn't know. His roving eyes, trained to find movement in mountains and forest, had determined there was nobody moving inside the room. Cautiously, he eased forward, fighting his fears.

"Are you crazy?" Alfred hissed from behind him. "Somebody'll see you!"

"We can't go back! Besides, I want to see this place up close."

Alfred approached carefully from behind. "I'm sure a person can't have a radio broadcast station without a permit from the government: Federal Communications Commission, in fact."

D.J. didn't know about that, but his mind was

beginning to focus on a possibility. "Maybe it's not a broadcast station at all, but only a control room of some sort. Hey! What's this?"

He spotted a small square box mounted in the wall near the far right wall and near the tunnel's ceiling. D.J. moved toward it.

"I think this is a speaker. A radio monitor."

He found a small knob under the unit and twisted it gently to the right. A terrible groan made both boys jump back.

"Now you've done it, D.J.!" Alfred hissed, his voice shaking.

D.J. glanced through the double thickness of glass window toward the slowly moving reels.

"You're hearing an audio tape played through that speaker. Probably coming from those reels transferring tape from one to the other. There's silence in between, and then more sound effects. Listen!"

The moaning stopped. The monitor was quiet a moment, then a single footstep sounded from the black box. D.J. felt his pulse speed up as he recognized something he'd heard before.

Alfred whispered, "Somebody's coming!"

D.J. shook his head. "No, it's on the tape again. More sound effects!"

Even though the boy said it, he felt fear begin to form goosebumps along his scalp, neck, shoulders, and arms.

It sounded exactly like the slapping slippers D.J. had heard outside his bedroom door! The boy's eyes roamed around the limestone ceiling, but there were no other monitors.

"Now I know how it was done, Alfred! I mean, how I heard the ghost walk! Somebody has placed a bunch of speakers—very small ones—inside the hallway walls and the ceiling of our bedroom. The tape here played through those stereo speakers in our room, making the footsteps seem to move across the room! Same with the moaning in the hallway."

He turned to face his friend whose eyes were wide and his mouth partly open. "It's not a regular broadcast station. It's only a control studio for sound effects. We've been hearing recorded sounds! There is *no* ghost!"

Alfred started to nod with relief, then stopped. "That might explain the sound, but what about what we *saw?* The light going across the yard and up to the tower balcony? The Chinese man's face with the funny hat? And what about the light you saw go through the third story door and vanish into a solid brick wall?"

D.J. blinked, his confidence shaken. But he refused to let his friend's fear reclaim him. D.J. shook his head. "I don't know—yet! But it's as I said before: there's no ghost! We know how the 'ghost' walks and moans! I don't know how it works so we can *see* it, but we'll find out!"

"If somebody doesn't grab us first," Alfred whispered, glancing around apprehensively. "Because even if there is no ghost, something sure happened to Kathy and your grandfather! They were in that tunnel, which probably means they were in this room too. But where are they now? We've disappeared just as they have!"

"Well, there's no way back, so we've got to go on.

Let's try that door into the room. There's probably another way out beyond those banks of electrical gadgets. Don't touch anything!"

D.J. heard Alfred making little muffled sounds of dismay, but the boys entered the room. It was well lighted but obviously fully automated. D.J. led the way cautiously around the center bank of electrical equipment, past glowing tubes behind glass and on to the other side.

"There!" He pointed. "A door on the left!"

"Where do you think it goes?"

"Let's find out." There was a small double-thick window about head-high in the thick door. D.J. peered through and saw stairs, faintly lighted from long fluorescent tubes mounted above the steps. He reached out and gently twisted the long silvery handle. He pushed carefully and the door swung silently outward.

His eyes probed upward. The steps were deeply carpeted. There was a handrail on each side of the steps. Both walls above the rails were filled with countless old posters and pictures right up to the ceiling. Every one of them featured an old-time radio microphone and faded 8" by 10" glossy photographs of people D.J. realized must have been broadcast stars a long time before television.

Alfred whispered behind D.J. "I recognize some of those names. I've heard the older folks at church talk about them! See? That poster's of 'The Lone Ranger'! That's one's 'The Whistler'! 'Gangbusters'! 'The Shadow'! There's one for—"

"I know!" D.J. interrupted. "All old-time radio drama programs! I've heard Grandpa talk about 'Amos 'n Andy,' 'One Man's Family', 'The Green Hornet,' and . . . 'Ma Perkins.' " His finger had been moving, pointing each out in turn. "I think she was a soap opera person way back in the old days."

"But how did these pictures get here?"

D.J. turned and faced his friend. "Miss Harridan! Remember when she was talking about what she used to do?"

Alfred thought a moment. "Yes—she was a radio actress! Before television! She said something about starting out in Hollywood as a radio actress. How did she put it? . . . 'We created a thousand worlds through the theater of the mind.' "

"Imagination!" D.J. agreed. "It's all done by making people's imagination create fear and things! That includes the ghostly moaning! Well, now we know who's behind this, Alfred. But we don't know why, or how we saw that . . . ghost—"

"Or where Grandpa and Kathy are!" his friend finished. "Up those stairs, maybe?"

D.J. took a deep breath. "Let's find out. Walk quietly and stay close to me."

The boys started up the steep stairs to a landing. It was about six feet square with a small upholstered chair resting in one corner. The stairs began again to the right.

D.J. tried to see all the way up the stairwell to the top, but there wasn't enough light. After a moment's rest, the boys climbed the second set of stairs to another landing.

"One more," D.J. whispered, "but let's stop and catch our breaths first."

Looking up, Alfred said softly, "It's apparently going to be on the third floor. But I thought you explored that . . . uh-oh!"

From the top of the stairs a door squeaked open. For a second, D.J. hoped it was only another sound effect, then he heard voices.

"They're coming down!" D.J. turned to whisper to Alfred. "Get back down the steps before they see us!"

The two boys turned and hurried down the deeply carpeted stairs as fast as they could. The voices behind suddenly stopped.

A man's voice demanded, "Who's there?"

There was no need to be quiet now. The boys clumped noisily down the stairs.

"Stop!" the voice called from behind. Heavy footsteps hurriedly descended the stairs behind them.

"Run!" D.J. whispered, reaching the control door and jerking it open for Alfred. "Straight ahead!"

The door closed behind them, deadening the sound of someone chasing after them. D.J. ran along the bank of panels.

"There's another door at the far end of the room! Let's see where it goes!"

He slid to a stop in front of the third door and took a quick peek through the small window. "More stairs! It's our only chance!"

The friends yanked the door open and rushed through. The door hissed softly shut, but it couldn't cut out the sound of yelling pursuit behind them.

The boys took this second set of stairs on fast tiptoes, hauling themselves up desperately by the rickety handrail. This stairwell was lighted only by a single bulb located about halfway up the landing. There were no posters on the bare wooden wall. It was obviously like a back door, with little use.

"Keep coming!" D.J. whispered hoarsely, fighting for breath. "Can't be any worse than what's behind!"

Both boys were panting hard when they reached the top and peered through a door with another small window in it. D.J. saw a tiny, round room with no windows. There was another door on the far wall, but no windows. D.J. felt sure this was the Witches Hat tower he'd seen from the outside of the mansion. A little portable electric heater glowed in the far corner with a cot in front of it.

"Grandpa!"

D.J. jerked the door open and raced across the room, Alfred right behind him. D.J. knelt by the old man who lay on the cot.

"Grandpa! It's D.J. Can you hear me?"

For a moment, there was no answer, and the boy was afraid he was too late. Then the old man stirred.

"D.J.? Is it really you?"

"It's really me! And Alfred! Are you all right?"

"I'm fine, except I'm all-fired tired of being kept in this here dinky little silo of a room!"

"D.J.?" The voice came from behind him. The boy whirled to see Kathy Stagg jumping up from another cot. "Oh, D.J.! I'm so glad to see you and Alfred!"

"You OK?"

"Just scared. I thought they'd get you too!"

Neither Grandpa nor Kathy were tied. D.J. glanced around the room, wondering why they hadn't tried to escape. His grandfather anticipated the boy's question.

"You see them there two doors? There's one you came through with them people between us and the outside. As for this door behind me: it opens out on a tiny balcony with no steps or anything down from it, and we're three stories up! And the door you came through can't be opened from the inside!"

In dismay, D.J. rushed to the door through which he and Alfred had come. There was a knob, but it wouldn't turn.

"You mean—we're prisoners too?"

Grandpa stood up with the use of his Irish shillelagh. "If I'd seen you boys a'coming, I'd a'warned you not to let the door close behind you."

D.J.'s mind spun crazily. He glanced around and realized the room had been soundproofed except for the wooden floor. For the moment, D.J. and Alfred had gotten away from their pursuers. However, it wouldn't take them long to figure out where the boys were. Any moment, D.J. expected to hear running feet pounding up the stairs where the boys had trapped themselves.

On the other hand, he and Alfred had found Grandpa and Kathy. But now all four of them were prisoners. Even if they could get the door open, Grandpa's arthritic hip would prevent him from moving fast, especially going down stairs. They couldn't expect to outrun their pursuers.

Alfred stepped close, interrupting D.J.'s whirling thoughts. "What're we going to do, D.J.? Nobody knows we're here! None of us will ever be found unless we—listen! They're coming up the stairs!"

Kathy grabbed D.J.'s arm. "Did you call somebody before looking for us?"

D.J. didn't answer but glanced desperately around the tiny room. Suddenly, he snapped his fingers.

"Hey! I've got an idea! Listen carefully and

everyone do exactly what I say!"

A minute later, the footsteps stopped just outside the door at the top of the stairs. Barely breathing, D.J. crouched behind the door with Alfred opposite him, pressed against the round wall.

D.J. heard a startled exclamation through the door, then it swung open.

"Now!" D.J. whispered.

Chapter Twelve

STRUGGLE IN THE WITCHES HAT ROOM

At D.J.'s whispered command, Grandpa let out a long, low groan. D.J. glanced at his grandfather. He lay in the middle of the tiny floor as though he had fallen. His left leg was on the cot. His right hand lay across the handle of his cane on the bare floor. Kathy knelt beside him, her back to the door where D.J. and Alfred crouched.

B.B. Shorqwat rushed through the open door. Miss Harridan stepped inside, but held the door open. Her eyes were on Grandpa and the ex-football player who shoved Kathy aside to bend over the old man.

Kathy stood up and took a quick step backward toward the open door.

Miss Harridan demanded, "What is it? Heart attack?"

"Don't know yet!" Shorqwat growled. "Hey, Old Man! What's the matter?"

D.J. was crouched so that all he had to do was

leap up. At the same instant, Alfred did the same from the other side of the open door. D.J.'s arm chopped down, knocking the housekeeper's hand from the door.

She jerked in surprise, and stumbled over Kathy who took another step toward the door. Miss Harridan, automatically drawing back from the boy's unexpected appearance, was off balance. She stepped back fast and fell across Shorqwat just as he started to jump to his feet.

Alfred grabbed the door to keep it from slamming shut. Kathy ducked under Alfred's arm and dove through the open door. A second later, Alfred followed her, blocking the door open from the outside with his hips.

D.J. didn't stop. He spun away from the doorway yelling, "Now, Grandpa!"

Grandpa jerked his leg off the cot and shoved himself to his feet with the aid of his cane. As the old man started hobbling rapidly toward the open door, Shorqwat reacted.

"No, you don't, you old buzzard!" The ex-football player shoved Miss Harridan aside as he grabbed for Grandpa's legs.

Grandpa, turning at Shorqwat's cry, swung his heavy cane backward and down in a chopping motion The blow caught Shorqwat across the forearm. He yelped and ducked as Grandpa thrust the cane down like a sword. He thrust it between the younger man's legs. Grandpa gave the cane a twist, and Shorqwat stumbled forward, his legs tangled. He tried to keep his balance. Grandpa flailed away with his cane, cracking shins and knees with a right good will.

"Try to mess with me, will ye?" he cried. "Here! Have some more of this here Irish shillelagh!"

D.J. called, "Enough, Grandpa!"

The football player howled and danced backward, trying to avoid Grandpa's flashing cane. Shorqwat tripped and fell heavily against the wall. He made a whooshing sound as his wind was knocked out of his chest. With a groan, he slid heavily to the floor.

"Come on, Grandpa! Get out! Please!"

Reluctantly, Grandpa lowered his cane and backed out the door which Alfred and Kathy were holding open. "That there feller's plumb out of condition, D.J.!"

D.J. helped Grandpa through the door while out of the corner of his eye, the boy saw Miss Harridan shove herself to her feet. She lunged for the door just as D.J. ducked through it.

"Close it! Close it!" D.J. cried, turning to help.

Four pairs of hands pulled the door shut hard. It clicked tightly into place just as Miss Harridan reached it.

For a moment, D.J. was looking through the small double thick pane of glass in the door—right into the housekeeper's blazing eyes. Her lips moved, and D.J. was glad he couldn't hear what she was saying.

"Boy!" Alfred breathed. "She's mad! Never saw her look like that before!"

"No," D.J. said softly, stepping back and taking a deep breath. "But we've never seen the *real* Miss Harridan before—just the ex-radio actress. Well, let's get out of here fast!"

He led the way down the stairs, followed by

Alfred, Kathy, and Grandpa. The old man was making remarkably good time with his cane and bad hip.

"Yippee!" he cried as D.J. led the way across the control room. "I ain't had me so much fun since I was knee high to a grasshopper's eye! Did you see how that there jasper went down when I tripped him with my Irish shillelagh? That'll teach him to mess with me!"

D.J. didn't answer. He hurried to the bottom of the staircase, past the control room equipment, and up the stairs where he and Alfred had been turned back a while ago by the sound of approaching voices.

"I sure hope they can't get out and catch us!" Kathy said.

"You and Grandpa couldn't get out and neither can they! Keep climbing! We've got to find a phone and call the sheriff!"

D.J. climbed the stairs past the old radio posters and photographs, slowing so Grandpa could keep up. The old man kept insisting they shouldn't wait for him.

D.J. reached the landing where there was a single door. He peered through the small window and shoved the door open.

Then he stopped. Kathy had been hurrying so fast she bumped into him. Alfred barely managed to avoid colliding with the girl. All three stood looking at a room of strange equipment. D.J. didn't have any idea what it was, but when Grandpa puffed through the door to join them, Alfred had the answer.

"I know!" he cried. "Holograms!*"

"Holo-what?" D.J. asked, still trying to catch his

breath.

"Holograms! I've read about them!" Alfred cried, hurrying to look over the assortment of strange equipment.

Grandpa snorted and waved his cane at the equipment. "Now I've done heard tell of telegrams and such, but what's this here hologram you're a'talking about?"

Alfred pushed his glasses up on his nose with an automatic thrust of his right thumb. "They're a true three-dimensional photograph! It's recorded on film by a reflected laser beam, as I remember. The subject is illuminated by a portion of the same laser beam."

Kathy protested, "I don't understand a word you're saying!"

"Me, neither!" Grandpa agreed, "but I've heard tell of them there lasers!"

D.J. didn't understand his best friend's technical explanation, but D.J. understood what was meant.

"You mean that what we saw wasn't real? The lamp the went across the lawn and up the outside wall? The Chinese man's face on the tower balcony?"

"Exactly!" Alfred replied. "Holograms! And that's how the light you saw on the third floor disappeared right into a solid brick wall! Nothing real—but holograms!"

D.J. smiled and clapped his friend on the shoulder. "Pictures! Lasers! Holograms! Alfred, that's just a visual counterpart to those sound effects!"

"Right, D.J.!"

"They almost made me believe in things I know don't exist! And all because of fear—what I *imagined* I heard and saw."

Kathy shook her head in bewilderment. "Well, you two can talk gibberish all night if you want, but I want to get out of this place—fast!"

D.J. turned to another door on the opposite side of the room. "Unless I'm badly mistaken, this should open onto—it does! The second floor! This is the wing where the boarders slept. We've just been in the end room that was always kept locked."

"I don't care about that!" Kathy cried, glancing down the gloomy hallway. "I know where we are now! There's a phone at the top of the stairs!"

"I'm on my way!" D.J. cried, sprinting down the hallway. A door opened and light spilled out of one room as he reached it. D.J. recognized Mr. Hatchett, the real estate salesman, still slipping a robe over his pajamas.

"What's going on?" he asked as D.J. raced on by.

"They'll tell you," he called over his shoulder.

D.J. heard a second door open. He turned his head enough to glimpse Mr. Grabnot, the promotion man in his bathrobe. The boy didn't wait for the man's question.

"Ask them!" he called without stopping. He slowed at the top of the familiar second story stairs, snatched the telephone off the wall and dialed the emergency number 911.

"Please get me the sheriff's office, fast!"

Chapter Thirteen

THE LAST SECRETS

Two days later, D.J. sat in the warm living room of the mansion and looked around. The people in the pictures still looked somberly out from their heavy carved frames, but everyone in the room was smiling.

D.J. saw Sheriff Cadwaller close his notepad and glance around the room with sad looking eyes.

"I think that about wraps up the last of my report," he said, standing up.

Miss Keene turned from the window where she had been looking out across the yard. "Did they tell you why they did it, Sheriff?"

"Well, originally Miss Harridan thought she had clear title to the mansion. But she didn't, and you bought the place. She'd thought that when she got the house all fixed up with sound effects and holograms, it'd be a big tourist attraction. Of course, she planned to let people know it was all done by tricks. And the Chinese ghost and the Civil War colonel's tunnel and secret rooms would be made public—so people would know it was all in fun.

"Miss Harridan needed help, of course, and that's where Shorqwat came in. Then, when you bought the place out from under her, Miss Harridan thought she'd use the electronic equipment to scare you off.

"But things got out of hand when Shorqwat caught Mr. Dillon looking around outside and took him prisoner without checking with Miss Harridan."

Grandpa growled and tapped his cane firmly on the carpeted floor. "I was right proud of myself! Walked plumb from town by myself, sneaked up along the riverbank—done it so good them noisy geese and guineas didn't even see me—and then ran smack dab into that football feller when I was a'trying to slip into the barn!"

The sheriff nodded. "You posed a real problem, Mr. Dillon. Mr. Shorqwat isn't too swift in the thinking department, so he grabbed you and hauled you off through the tunnel to that little room.

"Of course, Miss Harridan was furious when Shorqwat told her what he'd done, because they were suddenly involved with a kidnapping case, which is a federal offense. Later, when they saw you boys sneaking around, they tried to scare you off with the holograms and sound effects.

"Shorqwat didn't like taking orders from a woman, but Miss Harridan is a very strong-willed woman. She could do lots of things a man could—and took great pride in it—like wiring this house.

"She was some kind of a genius, I guess, because she dreamed up all that radio sound effects and the holograms. But you kids messed things up for her and Shorqwat."

Kathy shook her red-gold hair and smiled wanly. "I guess what really did it was when I had to take Smooch for a walk in the middle of the night. That's when I saw a little light from the Witches Hat tower. So I came back in, put Smooch in my room, and went looking—thinking it might be Grandpa Dillon."

D.J. muttered, "You should have called Alfred or me!"

"And let you think I was afraid?" Kathy cried. "Anyway, that's when Miss Harridan saw me. Naturally, I hadn't suspected her, so I told her about the light I'd seen. She said we'd go looking together. Only she took me to the basement and then into that room where Grandpa Dillon was a prisoner."

The sheriff nodded. "Kidnapping is a federal offense, and it wasn't something either of the parties responsible intended to do. Miss Harridan was so mad at Shorqwat when I talked to her last that she was trying to lay all the blame on him. He, of course, said it's all her fault. Between them, they'll talk themselves into a long prison term."

D.J. turned to the real estate man. "Mr. Hatchett, why'd you threaten Alfred and me out by the barn?"

"It wasn't a threat, boys! If you'll remember, I said, 'As a friend,' I'd advise you to get away. You see, I knew by then that something crazy was going on with the housekeeper and B.B. I didn't know what it was, but I felt sure you boys were in danger."

"You wrote the note and left it outside our door too?" Alfred asked.

"No," the sheriff answered. "Shorqwat did that in hopes you'd take off. He told me he and Miss Harridan were trying to decide what to do with Mr. Dillon here, and having you kids around complicated things."

Grandpa held up his cane to look at the end. "Can't get used to this here new rubber tip! Don't seem to me it makes near' as much noise as the old one!"

D.J. glanced at the old man. "Lucky you lost that old tip, Grandpa! We might never have found you!"

"You'd a'found me," he replied, thumping the cane across his shoe toe. "I tried to signal with it, a'tapping away on the floor every chance I got, hoping somebody'd hear me."

"I heard it," D.J. admitted. "But I wasn't sure it was you, and I couldn't tell where the sound was coming from."

"Well," the old man added, "one good thing done come out of this—I sure got caught up on my praying after that there football feller dragged me off like a sack of wheat!"

Sam Dillon had been sitting quietly, listening. "Seems to me that housekeeper was a strange one, all right. The sheriff here says she's like another person now—all bitter instead of nice like she was to us."

Mrs. Keene nodded. "She was an actress, all right. But she was talented in another way too. She rewired this place with B.B. Shorqwat's help! I was afraid of all the old electric wires in this place, so I let her do it. I probably should have been suspicious, but it never occurred to me that she would be using her abilities to create all this—ghost business."

Grandpa Dillon said, "Now, Ouida! Don't you go a'blaming yourself! That there housekeeper was just a plain greedy person with a dash of hatred thrown in! You never seen her be anything but nice, but she was meaner than a rattlesnake with me! Sure glad she's going to be a guest of the state for a long time."

D.J. saw Brother Paul sitting with his left leg crossed over his right. His big ten gallon Stetson was hooked over the left brown cowboy boot toe.

"Well, now," he said, his great voice booming out, "I'm mighty proud to be sitting here with you all instead of out there in my car, sicker than a horse, like last time."

Everyone laughed. Mrs. Keene reached over and patted the lay pastor's ham-like hand. "Brother Paul, you sure gave us a scare. But thank the Lord a little food poisoning can't keep you down."

"Well," Alfred said with a big grin, "I was worse off than you! Fear's a powerful thing!"

"Yes," D.J. said softly, thinking back. "I almost doubted God and nearly ended up believing in something that wasn't real. I mean, sound effects and holograms—my imagination was sure playing tricks on me!"

Brother Paul's voice rumbled up from his massive chest. "The Bible says, 'God has not given us a spirit of fear, but of power and of love and of a sound mind.' (2 Tim. 1:7). Reckon that's a good lesson for all of us to remember."

"Speaking of lessons," Mrs. Keene said, glancing at D.J., "how're you doing on your history composition?"

The boy grinned. "I've almost got it done! Wrote about some of the things we learned this week—the Chinese railroad workers, Devil's Law, and this mansion."

Alfred spoke up. "I've seen his rough draft, Mrs.

Keene, and I think you'll give him an 'A' for sure!"

"The main thing," D.J. said, "is that Mrs. Keene will have her bed and breakfast inn with more publicity than she'd ever have thought possible."

Grabnot, the promotion man, cleared his throat. "I'll help her too! We'll have the 'Moaning Mansion' known from coast to coast, and people will line up to stay here!"

The teacher's eyes misted. "You're all so kind! I thank God for such friends! But how can I thank you individually?"

"Well," D.J. said, glancing around, "I'd like to come here sometime, finish exploring this place in the daytime, and then finish out a good night's sleep without any ghostly noises and sights!"

Mrs. Keene smiled and reached out to lightly touch the boy's shoulder. "Consider it done! All of you will be my guests! And I'll personally see that the sound effects and holograms are disconnected for that whole night!"

Everyone laughed and applauded, including D.J. But as he glanced over at his best friend, D.J. almost wished he'd have another adventure that was as scary and yet so much fun.

Alfred leaned over and whispered, "D.J., if you're sorry this mystery is over, don't be! Knowing you, I'm sure you'll find some other adventure pretty soon!"

* * * * *

Alfred was right. Events were already shaping up for the boys to have another strange and exciting experience. Watch for the ninth D.J. Dillon

Adventure soon. It's called, **The Hermit of Mad River.**

LIFE IN STONEY RIDGE

ADOBE: Sun-dried bricks were very common in California even before the Gold Rush. Made of moist clay (as from a river), the dried bricks kept houses and stores warm in the winter and cool in the summer. Best of all, in Gold Rush towns that tended to have many terrible fires and little fire-fighting equipment, the adobe buildings would not burn.

ARMOIRE (Pronounced "Arm-**WAR**)**:** A large wardrobe or movable cupboard with shelves and doors.

BIBLIOGRAPHY: A list of reference books or other resources used in writing a paper or article.

CEDAR: An evergreen conifer, the deodar cedar is a fast-growing tree that reaches 80 feet with a spread of half that at the ground level.

CONIFERS: Another name for the many cone-bearing trees or shrubs. Spruce, fir, and pine trees are all conifers.

CUT-ACROSS DOG: Another name for a hair-pulling bear dog or heeler. The mixed breed dog does not trail with his nose on the ground as does a bloodhound or other trail hound. Instead, the cut-across dog runs with his nose in the air and "winds" the bear or other game when he's close.

DIGGER PINES: Growing up to 70 feet, these native California conifers are common in the western Sierra Nevada foothills. They are not good lumber trees. Their spare foliage is quite open instead of dense like ponderosas. The digger pine has a forked trunk and gray-green needles up to 13 inches long, which grow in clumps of threes. The large cones, up to 10 inches long, provided seeds which early Digger Indians used as an important food.

DUNCAN PHYFE (Pronounced "FIFE"): Furniture made in a particular style resembling that made by a Scottish-born American cabinetmaker by that name. The popular and simple design includes a lyre or a kind of harp in the back of a chair.

FORTY-NINERS: A term for men who came from all over the world to seek gold in California's Sierra Nevada foothills, starting in 1849.

FRET WORK: Angular designs or bands within a border as ornamentation.

GUINEA FOWL: A bird about the size of a chicken, originally imported from Africa for food and eggs. The fowls have dark-gray plumage spotted with white, and semi-bald heads somewhat resembling turkey vultures. Guinea fowl have a shrill, rocking cry.

HAIR-PULLER: A small, quick dog of mixed breed. The hair-puller's natural tendency is to go for the heels or backside of any animal, including sheep, cows, or bears. This mutt is also called a "heeler" or "cut-across" dog.

HIGH BOYS: Another name for tall chest of drawers with legs.

HOLOGRAM: A true three-dimensional photograph recorded on film by a reflected laser beam of a subject illuminated by a portion of the same laser beam.

IRISH SHILLELAGH (Pronounced "Shuh-**LAY**-Lee")**:** A cudgel or short, thick stick often used for a walking cane. A shillelagh is usually made of blackthorn saplings or oak and is named after the Irish village of Shillelagh.

LIQUIDAMBAR: A member of the sweetgum family, this slender tree is wide at the bottom and tapers to a pointed top. The star-shaped leaves turn magnificent shades of red and yellow each autumn before falling.

LIVE OAK: Interior live oak is a handsome tree growing up to 75 feet tall. This tree is common in the lower mountain areas and foothills of California's Sierra Nevada Mountains. It has a rounded crown and wide-spreading branches. An evergreen, the live oak does not shed its leaves in winter.

MADRONE: A beautiful evergreen tree that grows to a height of about 80 feet. The pinkish-orange hardwood makes excellent firewood, though it doesn't usually split as evenly as oak does.

MOTHER LODE: A term applied to the gold-bearing area in the foothill section of California's Sierra Nevada Mountains running from about Mariposa on the south (near Yosemite) to Downieville in the north. The famous Gold Rush of 1849 covered this area. Many people still find gold today in the Mother Lode.

OL' SATCHELFOOT: An outlaw bear that was told about in the first D.J. Dillon adventure, **The Hair-Pulling Bear Dog.**

PASTORAL: Simple and serene, like pastures and related items in a peaceful, rural countryside.

PONDEROSA: Large North American trees used for lumber. Ponderosa pines usually grow in the mountain regions of the West and can reach heights of 200 feet. The ponderosa pine is the state tree of Montana.

PRISCILLA CURTAINS: A double row of curtains suspended over a window from two overhead rods and tied back about halfway down. This creates an opening in the lower part of the curtains. Priscilla curtains are usually made of lacy material and have ruffled edges.

RED MAPLES: One of the more popular deciduous shade trees planted in the California foothills, the broad leaves turn a blazing scarlet color in the autumn.

RIGHT GOOD WILL: A common expression meaning enjoyment or a strong desire to do something.

SANK SHAFTS: When miners dug into the earth to search for underground veins of gold, they used the term "sank" instead of digging. What they made was called a shaft. It was a vertical or inclined excavation or opening from the surface.

SIDEBOARD: A piece of furniture, sometime with shelves and drawers to hold table service in a dining room.

STETSON: A broad-brimmed, high-crowned felt hat like a cowboy's. The Stetson is named for John B. Stetson, an American hatmaker who lived during the time of the Old West.

SUGAR MAPLES: A popular deciduous shade tree planted in the California foothills. In the fall, the 6-inch wide leaves turn colors from spectacular yellow-orange to deep red or brilliant scarlet.

SUGAR PINE: Largest of the pine trees. Sugar pines

can grow as tall as 240 feet. They have cones that range from 10 to 26 inches long which are often used for decorations.

VALLEY OAKS: An oak that drops its leaves in winter, this largest of all such trees in California grows in the central valleys up into the foothills. It may take several shapes from rounded and graceful, to tall and upright.

WINCHESTER HOUSE: A 160-room Victorian mansion with stairs that go nowhere and doors that open to bare walls. The house has forty-seven fireplaces, three working elevators, and 10,000 windows. One of the windows is in the floor. Widowed Sarah Winchester, eccentric heiress to the Winchester Rifle fortune, began construction of the mansion in 1884. Building continued around the clock for thirty-eight years until Mrs. Winchester died. The mansion is open to the public at San Jose, near San Francisco, California.

The Hair-Pulling Bear Dog
D.J.'s ugly mutt gets a chance to prove his courage.

The Bear Cub Disaster
When his pet bear causes trouble in Stoney Ridge, D.J. realizes he can't keep the cub forever.

Dooger, The Grasshopper Hound
D.J. and his buddy Alfred rely on an untrained hound to save Alfred's little brother from a forest fire.

The Ghost Dog of Stoney Ridge
D.J. and Alfred find out what's polluting the mountain lakes—and end up solving the ghost dog mystery.

Mad Dog of Lobo Mountain
D.J. struggles to save his dog's life and learns a hard lesson about responsibility.

The Legend of the White Raccoon
Is the white raccoon real or only a phantom? As D.J. tries to find out, he stumbles upon a dangerous secret.

The Mystery of the Black Hole Mine
D.J. battles "gold" fever, and learns an eye-opening lesson about his own selfishness and greed.

Ghost of the Moaning Mansion

Will D.J. and Alfred get scared away from the moaning mansion before they find the "real" ghost?

The Secret of Mad River

D.J.'s dog is an innocent victim—and so is the hermit of Mad River. Can D.J. prove the hermit's innocence before it's too late?

Escape Down the Raging Rapids

D.J.'s life depends on reaching a doctor soon, but forest fires and the dangerous raging rapids of Mad River stand in his way.